AFTERNOON OF THE DINOSAUR

by

Cristina Peri Rossi

Translated by

Robert S. Rudder and Gloria Arjona

CRISTINA PERI ROSSI

Cover illustration by John Seymour

ISBN-13: 978-0615955636 (SVENSON Publishers)
ISBN-10: 0615955630

To Laureano Mota

and to my little nephew, Pablo,

just in case during his afternoons

dinosaurs occasionally appear.

.

CONTENTS

PROLOGUE

INVITATION TO ENTER A HOUSE

By

Julio Cortázar

On the day that someone comes out with the definitive anthology of the fantastic tale, it will be seen that many of those stories that forever dwell in the fearful memory of the genre take place around a house, are an emanation of it, in some way bear an invitation to cross over the threshold, so that afterward the protagonist reader may discover for himself other doors not constructed in carpentry shops during the daylight hours of the city.

It is no accident that books of stories such as this are in themselves one of those inner houses, and that each tale offers a passage through rooms, galleries, patios and stairways that draw the reader in and separate him from his former world. It could be said that writers like Cristina Peri Rossi repeat unknowingly (but what is knowing in this no-man's-land where dinosaurs and queen bees roam) the dark archetype of Bluebeard's castle: rooms, corridors with mirrors, boarded up or forbidden doors, doors—always— for those who would rather face horror and death than abandon their efforts to open them. One story ends and others begin in the next room; powerless to resist, with the fingers of our eyes we will once again seek out the lock, the hasp, we will push against the swinging doors and we will see.

We will see children. For years Cristina's stories have woven their slow, spiraling circles around children until they have suffocated them or been suffocated by them. Because we should not forget that Bluebeard is Mr. Gilles de Rais, and that the forbidden door opens into the crypt of ultimate sacrifices, that of Huysmans, of *Là-bas*, that of the savage and perfumed music of Bartók. In this old new house, in this recurrence of the interminable ceremony, the children are witnesses, victims and judges of those who sacrifice them as they beget them, raise them, love them, clothe them, delegate them. Once before, in a tale from years back, *La rebelión de los niños* (*The Children's Rebellion*), Cristina had entrusted to juvenile hands a lustral task that adults are not always capable of carrying out. In three of the stories from this new book the children will lay bare the world of those who claim to control it, and will reduce it to a laughingstock of truth. Just as in *Cría cuervos* (*Raise Crows*), the Carlos Saura film, the lone gaze of childhood shatters forever a society that obstinately persists in denying what is.

But adolescence emerges, slowly and bitterly; in that turbid interlude the games enter a territory where Cristina recognizes and takes on the sealed door, the interdiction that will be violated, the horrible conciliation of victims and assassins. Brothers and sisters, queens and slaves, false adults incapable of accepting the laws of the game, people that an Aubrey Beardsley or an Egon Schiele would have drawn with the perverse perfection of sterile desire, of a pursuit whose sole incentive is that of *not* catching the prey, whether it be named Patricia or Alexandra, Igor or Alina. False adults, for the simple reason that adults are false. And the adolescent turns to its past in a last, desperate act of resistance; but its sex and its hair and its voice drag it to the peak that the boy of the dinosaur contemplates in final horror. Now there are no victims or assassins in those rooms of the house; the last of its visitors is able only to utter one useless word: *Mercy*.

All of that has been lived and told by a woman who knows the hells of this earth – hers, there in the south –

and those of the written word in our day – here, everywhere. Her beautiful choice is to project onto imaginary planes a historical content, tragically real, that not only retains its most precise meaning, but multiplies its force in the other imagination, that of the reader who now enters the house, who stretches out his hand to the first door, of course forbidden, of course fascinating, that opens into a cell where, at the far end, is a second door, of course forbidden, of course fascinating.

FROM BROTHER TO SISTER

Every time I look at my sister I think of Mama. And I know that deep down I wish my mother had been her, my sister, and not herself, perhaps if my mother could have been my sister I wouldn't notice the difference so much. Every time I look at her, every single time. I put on a record, I look out the window, the room is bare, only the photographs I've put up on the wall, females in shades of black and white, delicate poses to conjure up dreams, meditations, a woman—exquisite, slender—softly stretching, like a feline, head unseen, only the stylized lines of her body, it's a striking photograph, I don't know how many prizes it's won, and I bought the "Photographer's Annual" and there it was, along with other beautiful photographs of women, they wouldn't all fit in the room, when I look at them I think of sweet, sensual things, taking photographs, writing poems, loving a sister, each separately, and then all of them together. I want to photograph Alina, nude. I have asked her, and I continually ask her, every day. When she comes out of the bath and leaves a trail of water that I like to follow, like a dog, savoring the drops, I kneel down on the floor and I lick them up, Alina laughs, she musses my hair, she calls me a monster, her monster (her monster?, perhaps, perhaps, no, I know quite well), I lick the drops one at a time because I can't lick the skin, I insist on the photograph.

We were on the beach. I was watching her face. Her face, nothing but her face. I'll keep the pleasures separate. That afternoon—the sky, the color of lilac, the water, rough, retreating in calm turbulence, the three of us alone, walking this way and that way along the shore, coming and going, throwing driftwood into the water, stones, sand, a sinister screeching of birds overhead, augurs of rains and deceit—I decided to begin with her face. Later I would concentrate on her very long legs. She had a small stone in her hand, I positioned myself to one side, to especially appreciate her profile, she laughed, Mario was running around her like a young puppy, as though drunk, she was tolerating him, I put up with him even though he was annoying me a little, she was whirling around, the wind playing with her hair, for she preferred to dance, she threw the stone—far, I felt the pain of an object destroyed, I was the fugitive stone swallowed up by the water, why did you release me, why from your hand through the air to the sea, you don't know the pain you've caused me, she picked up another stone, but this time she held it in her hands.

"Thank you very much," I said to her, "I wouldn't have been able to endure being thrown again." In her warm hand the stone did not feel rough.

She looked at it, understanding, caressed it. "It wasn't intentional," she told me, "I didn't mean to hurt you." At that same instant I took another photograph of her. A close-up of her very long legs walking, her slight bust, delicate neck, her head moving in the wind, all of it together, a rhythmical lasciviousness, the silence of a panther, lazy lustfulness, in the background the sea pulling back, blue, frightened, low clouds, black birds circling.

Meanwhile Mario was putting pieces of driftwood in the water and then taking them out again. That languid face of Alina driving the student mad. In back of the madness of her hair, the exercise with driftwood. Against the suggestion of her legs moving, of her arms as they are raised, endless swimming. And Mario puts in another piece of wood, and with all the candor of a sports fan he says to me: "Isn't she something?" And I despise him, Mario, the face of a slow student, the face of a good tennis player, Alina has burrowed into your thoughts like some strange animal, an equation difficult to solve, you will fail your exam, poor Mario, torn with anxiety you will go to the tribunal, driveling the meager bits of knowledge you've picked up during afternoons at the beach like this one, that are foreign to you, you will approach, trembling, in a vain attempt to master the craft, the proper language, the academy has been of no use, the wood will founder with you, one, two, three, how many pieces of driftwood have you dragged over this afternoon without her even bothering to glance at you, know this well, she is walking in the sand, thinking only of herself, I am taking photographs of her, she is my sister, something dark we two share because we have been summoned before a judge in the same grotto, something forbidden to you, something you will never know or be a part of, Mario the athlete, brawny Mario, she has not noticed your muscles, wrapped up as she is in herself.

I will not help you during the test, when she examines you and laughs pitifully at your torso, at your arms, at your impeccable swimming form, and the battle will leave you crushed, you don't know about the cruelty of battle, when she can crush you and overpower you, barely moving, fixing her gaze on you, stony eyed, looking at you and laughing, Hercules, and you will collapse beside her, you will chew sand in defeat, you will follow her around the beach, crawling, she may let a few drops from her bathing suit fall on your head, and you will be sorry that you did not have your mouth open so that you could drink them. You will drink the strange juice from her clothing. You will go into her tent when she is not there, to touch her pants, smell her bathing suit. And night will come upon you as you rummage through her clothing, the way an old actor goes through the rags he still has, the castoffs, something to possess, to hold onto. Mario the abandoned, the ignored, the forsaken, the ridiculed.

"Alina, your profile."

Obedient, like a docile, dark animal, she turns and looks toward the eye of the camera as it follows her.

"Are you tired?" I ask her, as gently as possible. Mario mistakes the driftwood for algae and complains that lichens are invading his fishing poles.

I have been looking at her footprints. Whenever she takes a step the sand scarcely flattens under her foot, that contact, it gives way, softly, I have placed my hand in the small impression. I've left my hand there, as though on her sex organ.

"Get up," she says to me, sister to brother. I shall never forget that sinuousness of sand.

Din 21, 100 ASA, diaphragm: 5.6; speed 60. She is standing still now, like a print, Din 21, we are married, when we were small we pretended we were married, ASA 100, it's not the same now, by the window grating Mama was angry, aperture 5.6, how will she spread her legs?

"Alina, spread your legs."

Please. Open your legs, speed 60, Din 21, ASA 100, diaphragm 5.6, what do you do when I'm not around? Hercules is looking at you too. He knows nothing. He has never played with you at night when he was a child, nor hidden among the trees with her, helped her to dress, your clothing too, I am going to photograph your clothing, but more than anything, I would like to photograph you, nude.

"Wait a minute, I'm tired," and Alina, giddy, throws herself on the ground to rest. I play with the camera like a cat, I take out the film, I turn it around in my hands, I end up sitting next to her, touching her leg. A long, painful caress. Painful because it is slow, timid, cowardly. I am touching the hem of her pants, the side that is sewn, the seam that ends at her foot.

Mario comes over to sit with us.

"We're going to put up posters at midnight," he tells us.

I would rather not go: I want to photograph Alina, nude. Alina painting handbills. Alina pasting up posters, and the sirens screaming. Who will protect her?

"I'm going with you," I tell her.

She turns, playful, amused, she runs her fingers through my hair.

"I'll have enough protection. It will be your turn tomorrow."

I'll go with you. Sitting in the truck, silent. We'll get down quickly, with the buckets, brushes, the posters we have to put up. One will stand guard. One or two. But I'll be with you while you, happy and unconcerned, paste our posters on buildings. Down with tyranny, long live liberty. A homeland for all or a homeland for none. And the sirens will wail as they come closer. Who will turn us in this time? But I'll be at your side. And Mama, waiting for us, dinner ready. "Was it a good guitar concert?" she'll ask, and you will talk vaguely about Rodrigo and Father Soler. I will watch you, shivering, because night is coming on and the rooms are separate, because without warning we grew up. Without warning we grew up and no one could stop it, I, the pilot's best student, you the most beautiful. And Mama, repeating that we were very late. You have a slight cut on your hand. You scratched yourself when you ran to the truck and Mario used his handkerchief and I accidentally overturned the bucket of paint that was left. And you said it was nothing. I had placed the camera under some newspapers to protect it. I can't leave you at home, as if I were your husband, that's why I have to go along with you. Although Mario doesn't understand, and there are so many times when he wonders what we are thinking, and when your hand was bleeding you looked at me, terrified, and I looked at you and I took your hand, I said to you, "Don't worry, it's nothing," and Mario held out his handkerchief to me and then you smiled at me, because I was holding your hand and you said, "That's right, it's nothing," and you nearly, very nearly, promised me the photograph. "That obsession with photographs," Mama says. "If only you could use it for something." It does have a use when we go to a wedding, Alina, Mario and I, and while we are smothering our laughter at the old folks posing and the clothing, I use up one or two rolls of film that, later, the family will pay for handsomely. Blow-ups, 9x10, some even larger. Mario uses the occasion to drink whiskey if they have any, Alina strolls along the house's balconies and gardens. "Look at that moon," she says to me, or "You can see the ocean from here," she exclaims and, between snapping photos, I run sweetly over to touch her. How I would love her on those estates that are not ours, that are beyond our class, and how I love her in our tiny houses without gardens or balconies.

Suddenly I say, "Let's go," and the beach, the house, the balcony, the street, the square, the movie-theater, the pond are left empty, a beach without Alina, a house without lights, a distant balcony, a funereal street, a deserted square, a closed-down movie theater, an empty pond, all without you.

And the student comes with us.   He leaves the driftwood behind, he picks up the fishing-poles, he walks more slowly, weighed down by the things he is carrying; the two of us going on ahead, Alina is tired, her hand hurts a little, she leans on my shoulder, Mario shouts, "Wait for me," she whispers to me "Let's leave him behind," or was it I who whispered those words?, I can manage her, I could lift her like a feather because I've grown so much since we slept in the same room, I can take her by the waist, lift her, hold her, and start running with her in my arms, run away, leave the beach behind forever, the square, Mama, the institute, pasting up handbills at night, the excuses, the memories, then I take her by the hand, I help her run, she laughs in delight, Mario is left further and further behind, carrying the poles; holding her hand, I make her run faster, my camera is hanging down on the other side, she is exhilarated, I feel excited, we can barely see the student, we no longer hear his cries, when we have run far away she suddenly stops me:

"Where is Mario?" she asks.

I nudge her with my arm, I make her start running again, we run very quickly, in the rush she insists:

"I think I hear him shouting," she says to me.

"No, Alina, it's the birds, it's only the birds," I tell her, and I am certain that this time I will really photograph her nude.

AT THE BEACH

Water pounded against rocks, foam rose into the air, lapping at stones. The scene was perfect because there were lights in the church and the moon was full. They had come to the resort two days earlier, had taken a room in a three-star hotel where the window opened onto the beach, and they had no complaints about the food. They got up early, ate breakfast, and went down to the sand. It was brown and powdery, rather heavy and sticky, and it was difficult to find an empty spot where they could set up their things. The canvas awnings were all crowded together, and there was no privacy. At least within the limits of decency, which they had no intention of defying. They seldom wanted to defy anyone or anything. They felt, instinctively, that by respecting the most general norms, they were keeping themselves free of the dangers that threatened dissidents, those who lived on the edge, fugitives, nonconformists. They also thought their mild, respectful attitude had its reward: those twenty days of vacation at a fashionable seaside resort were their reward for being obedient, for obeying the law. From a distance they looked like brother and sister. Blond, with clear eyes, delicate skin, conservative clothing, soft-spoken, they walked hand in hand along the beach, and they were the sort of people who were never caught by the afternoon breeze without a coat in their bag, just in case. This sort of cautiousness allowed them to stay at the seaside until sunset on this day, when the strong evening mist drove nearly everyone else away. They also felt fortunate that their reward for being sensible was this marvelous sunset. He tossed a grey sweater that his mother had knitted for him over his shoulders, she put on a blue one she had picked up at a clearance sale. Warmed by the wool, they looked out at the sea and the explosion of sun as it bled across the horizon. He focused on it from a distance, and shot the sun. He killed it instantly. Satisfied, he advanced the film.

"The perfect crime," she said.

"No, dear, a rather dirty piece of work: a few spots of blood spoil the picture. You can buy a crime like this very cheaply at any store where they sell postcards, but it's the sort of thing a person always tends to commit alone."

The beach was empty, everyone had disappeared at the first sign of wind; people love getting a sunburn, but they can't bear the thought that they might catch cold. There was just one little girl in a white dress, playing in the sand. She wasn't building castles because the sand seemed very fine, and she wasn't using her shovel to draw outlines of princesses or horses or astronauts either: she was simply looking at the two of them. She was solitary to an extreme, and couples always made her curious: until this moment she had never felt the need to share silence, the sunset, bathing, anything.

"That little girl must be lost," remarked the woman. "The poor little thing, let's call her over and find out who her parents are."

"Be careful, Alicia," he answered. "Children these days can be dangerous."

There was a breach between the generations. The Pope, the Church and the Military had already noticed it. Probably a mix-up in the genes. Parents had resembled their children for centuries. Nowadays it was hard to find any parent who looked like his or her child. Inexplicably, this rift was blamed on the children. The disturbance could have been caused by the atomic bomb, failed revolutions, pollution or the influence of movies. Or it could have been the food. People were eating at home less and less; they would rather eat fried eggs and sausage at an Automat or in a restaurant. It was one of those factors, or it was all of them together, like cancer.

"Little girl," Alicia called out sweetly.

The sun grew faintly redder. He set the camera, caught the right angle and shot again. Click. He looked at his camera, not really convinced that it had done a good job. He had already killed several landscapes, but still he wasn't satisfied. His vacations were so perfect, he would certainly never forget them: he took photographs to remember. Who could trust his own memory?

"Honey," insisted Alicia.

The child looked at them skeptically. Slowly she turned her head away, she felt that the landscape was more deserving of her attention, and she concentrated on contemplating the sea.

"She must be a foreigner, she probably doesn't understand our language," remarked Alicia.

"They're *all* foreigners," he said, trying to remove the film from the camera.

Startled, she looked at him. Sometimes he said things that, on the surface, had a clear meaning, but still turned out to be ambiguous, doubtful, and there was nothing that made her feel worse than ambiguity. What did he mean? That everyone on the beach was a tourist? That all children spoke another language? That childhood was like being from another planet?

"I don't think so. She looks completely normal," she assured him.

"Don't think that all foreigners have dark skin and wide noses," he added.

Anyway, despite her husband's indifference, she wanted to find out for herself. She thought it was terrible for anyone to leave a little girl alone on the beach at this hour. If the two of them hadn't been there—and they were there because, being thoughtful and well organized, they had planned ahead and put two sweaters in the beach bag—the child might surely have come to some harm at the hands of degenerates who roamed the shoreline at dusk. The newspapers always had stories about things like that happening in foreign countries, and the fact was, the resort was full of foreigners. Or she could have drowned. Some children have no sense of survival, they're like little animals.

"I wonder where her parents are?" she said to herself, aloud. She didn't look like an orphan. There were fewer orphans all the time, at least in the world they lived in. That was almost certainly due to advances in medicine that were prolonging men's lives. And women's even more, since they had fewer vices.

"At the pool, or drinking whiskey in the hotel bar," he snorted. He had attached the flash because he wanted to take some pictures of his wife, even though there wasn't enough sunlight now.

"You'll have to get some copies made to send home," she remarked. "Home" was still her parents' home. Her grandparents' home. Her uncles and aunts' home. She liked to send them color photographs of their marvelous vacations.

"If the child would come closer, I'd take some pictures of her," he said. "I've seen some exceptional photographs of children, taken by amateurs."

"Honey," his wife called again. She didn't want to move because she secretly loathed walking through the damp evening sand.

Surprisingly, the girl got up of her own volition, completely aware of her gestures and movements. As though she had completed some task satisfactorily, and was now getting ready to leave. As though she had carried out a mission, and felt a sense of pleasure along with the sort of emptiness that suddenly takes over afterward.

"Have her come closer, I'll take her picture," he said.

She didn't pick anything up because she had nothing to pick up, nor did she look back, because she was leaving nothing behind, and she walked straight toward them. Her little white dress was blowing in the wind.

"The poor thing, she finally understood, and she's coming to us for protection. She must be lost, and I know she has to be cold in that little white dress."

The girl covered the distance quickly, and stopped near them. She stood there, watching them curiously, with a steady gaze. They were both sitting down, and when he pressed the shutter, he saw that the flash wasn't charged. The girl took no notice of this mishap. Still standing, she put a finger in her mouth. It was a robust, intelligent finger: with its rosy tip, she had come to know the world and to love it. Sometimes it tasted like honey, like fresh apples, like dust, like thyme, sometimes it tasted like lemon, and it had taught her to stay away from hot things and from people with rough, chapped skin. Alicia was nervous because she knew what a temper her husband had when a photograph didn't turn out, or when it turned out badly. The girl took advantage of the woman's nervousness, and with a firm, resolute voice, she asked them:

"What country are you from?" with a perfect accent, but one that revealed it was not her native language.

"We're from here," the woman answered in surprise.

The girl came right up to them, carefully examining the skin on her arms. Alicia shuddered uncomfortably, feeling that she was being given a thorough inspection. Her skin was covered with freckles, and the girl seemed to want to touch them, to see them close up. Her husband was still fiddling with the flash attachment. The child came even closer, and she could smell her iodine scent, her sea scent, and when she had her little nose right over the freckles on her arms, she asked politely:

"What are those things?"

"What are what things?" Alicia nearly shouted, indignant. "They're freckles, haven't you ever heard of freckles?"

"They don't have insects like that in my country," the girl said, reaching out to touch them.

Alicia motioned her away in disgust. This frightened the child a little, but her interest was immediately rekindled, and she extended her hand again. This time, though, she asked permission:

"Can I touch them?"

She couldn't understand why foreigners never taught their children to respect adults.

"No," answered Alicia bitingly.

The girl did not insist. Her considerable disdain for Alicia was apparent, and she simply remarked:

"When the sun comes up again, I'll look along the shore for insects like those. The sand is full of them. Why is that man taking pictures?"

He jumped, startled, when he heard the child's voice so close to his ear. He had been preoccupied, trying to figure out what was wrong with the flash, and he hadn't heard what they were saying.

"Is she lost or not?" he asked his wife, ignoring the child's curiosity.

"I don't know," she said. "She's a foreigner."

"For a foreigner, she speaks our language pretty well," he commented.

"All children can do that. I think they find our language very beautiful."

"No," said the child, interrupting what they had thought was a private conversation. "I asked why that man is taking pictures. I don't like the way you people say 'horse', and I don't like the way you say 'watch' either. Why do you have sweaters?"

"Where are your parents?" asked Alicia, trying not to answer.

"At home," the child immediately responded. "If that machine kills the sun, I'll throw it in the water."

"Little girl," said the man, "if you want, we'll take you back to your house. Wouldn't you like that? Aren't you cold?"

"I'm never cold," she replied. "Cold is old. Will it kill the sun, or not?"

"Haven't you ever seen a camera?"

"She's a foreigner," interjected Alicia, now that the girl was talking to her husband. "Probably from India. There might not be any cameras where she lives, or maybe they're hard to find."

"I have a cat that you don't," the child interrupted.

"A *cat*?" cried Alicia, in dismay. She couldn't stand pets. Or any other kind of animal either.

"That's impossible," said her husband. "No country's that backward these days. There can't be more than a few primitive tribes left that don't know what a camera is."

"If you want me to, I'll bring him here," offered the child. She seemed to be willing to make concessions.

"Don't even think of it," said Alicia in alarm. "We'll take you home and then you can feed your kitten."

"It's not a kitten," said the child. "It's a baby-cat. And besides, it's here on the beach with me."

"So that's the reason the sand on this beach is so dirty," mused Alicia. "Kitten and baby-cat are synonyms, child. Do you know what synonyms are?" She didn't wait for an answer, but explained: "Two words that mean the same thing."

"There aren't any sin-omins," said the little girl. "They're all different."

"They sound different, but they can have the same meaning."

"There aren't any sin-omins," she insisted. "Everything is different."

"She's stubborn as a mule," he blurted out irritably.

"Children are all alike," mused Alicia.

"They're all different," the girl assured her. Was she still talking about synonyms or about children now?

"Where do you all sleep?" she asked suddenly.

"At our hotel," Alicia answered proudly.

"The little insects," said the girl, looking at her arm again.

"I've already told you, they're not insects. Don't you understand?"

"The hotel doesn't belong to you."

"What hotel?"

"That one where you sleep. You said: 'Our hotel.'"

"We rent a room there," answered the husband.

"You seem to put a lot of importance on language," said the wife.

"I can bring my little cat here and show him to you," the girl offered again.

"That won't be necessary," she said, trying to dissuade her. "We'll see him some other day."

"There isn't any other day," answered the child.

"Of course there is! Look: we've made reservations at the hotel for two more weeks."

"If he kills it, there won't be another day."

"I've never killed the sun," he said with a smile.

"The cat," the child clarified.

"I don't like cats, but I'd never kill one," he protested.

"It's the same thing," she insisted. "He would die. I have lots of them. In different houses."

"You see?" she said. "This child's parents are divorced. That's why she's confused. I don't know why people even have children."

"To perpetuate the species," the child responded very calmly. Speechless, they both looked at her in wonder. She had answered them as though reciting from a manual.

"Do you know what 'perpetuate the species' means?" he asked her in a surprised tone.

"Yes," she said, very satisfied that she had answered the way they taught her at school.

"All right, let's see, tell us what it means."

"I don't want to," she said.

"You don't know," he replied.

"No, it's because I don't want to. I want to show you my little cat."

"It's because you don't know."

"It's because I don't want to."

"Anibal, leave that child alone. Let's take her back to her house, or to the hotel or somewhere."

"Why do both your names begin with A?"

"How can we find out where she lives? She doesn't seem very inclined to answer," he submitted.

"Mine begins with an E."

"And what's the rest of it?" he asked her. Maybe he could get some identification.

"Euuuuyllarre," the girl answered.

"That's not a name. It doesn't mean anything."

"It means what I want it to," she declared. She had read that somewhere.

"And what does it mean right now?"

"Euuuuyllarre," answered the girl.

"That doesn't mean anything. It's not a name. It's something you made up."

"That's what I want my name to be right now," she explained.

"And when you don't want people to use that name, what do they call you?"

"Whatever they like."

"Let's not start in again," said Alicia.

"If you don't want to see my cat, I have another one," she said proudly.

"We don't want to see that one or the other one," interrupted Alicia.

"Well then, I'll show you still another one."

"Not that one either," he said.

"What about the cat that's the other cat even after that cat?"

"It seems to me you're giving yourself more cats than you really have."

"It seems to me that you don't like cats very much."

"Nor little girls, either," he replied irritably.

"My poppa doesn't either," she said.

"He doesn't like little girls or cats?" he asked.

"He likes the cat, but not the other one."

"Where is your poppa?" Alicia tried to coax from her.

"In the pen."

"Don't you mean in the den?"

"I mean in the pen."

"He must be one of those foreigners that's always getting drunk every night at the hotel bar."

"And your mamma?" insisted Alicia.

"Which one?" she asked.

"How many mothers do you have?" she asked in wonder.

She seemed to think for a moment, looked at her fingers, made some calculations in the air, and then answered:

"Just one."

"Where does she live?"

"At home," she answered.

"And where is she now?"

She began to play in the sand.

"She was at the beach a while ago," answered the child.

"And she left you all alone?" asked Alicia in horror.

"No. I left her alone to play with the cat."

"Where did you leave her?" asked the husband.

"In the pen."

"We'll never get anywhere this way," said Alicia, who was starting to be concerned. "Maybe if we offer her something. It's easy to win children over with food."

"Would you like a sandwich?" posed the husband.

"I already ate," said the child.

"You can eat again, if you'd like."

"No. I don't want to be fat like you."

"I'm not fat," he protested.

"You don't move around enough, you'll get fat."

"Who told you I don't move around?"

"The sand. It doesn't move when you don't."

"I've moved around enough for today."

"Why don't you start moving for tomorrow?" she asked with complete innocence.

"I don't want to. I like to do things in their own time."

"What time?" the little girl asked.

"The appropriate one."

"I don't know," said the child.

"What don't you know?"

"What time 'appropriate' is."

"There isn't any time called 'appropriate'. I said I like to do things in their time."

"Whose?"

"Whose what?"

"Whose time."

"The one for each thing. Each thing has its own time."

"How do you know?"

"Because, unlike you, they taught me when I was little."

"What's her time?" asked the child, pointing at Alicia.

He was left speechless. He had never thought about it. He set himself to imagining appropriate responses, like: "Her time is always." "Her whole life." "It's the time of dawn and summer." The time of action or of meditation? The domestic time or perhaps another dimension, less habitual? He had to make a choice between two vague replies: all of them, or none.

"Her time is all time," he declared finally, quite satisfied with the phrase he had made up. Proudly, she lifted her head a little.

"If you don't want to see my cat, it must not be my cat's time."

"We don't care whether it's your cat's time or not, it's hers and mine."

"Broad and Alien is the World," said the little girl thoughtfully, looking at the sky. He had the irritating sensation that he didn't know whether she was pulling their leg or if she was serious.

"Where did you pick up that beautiful phrase?" he asked ironically.

"In school. It's an old book. All the books at school are old."

"What do you think it means?"

"Nothing. That broad and alien is the world."

"You're repeating yourself."

"There aren't any sin-omins, and I'm against interpretation."

"What do you mean, you're against interpretation?"

"My father has a book called 'Against Interpretation'."

"What did I tell you?" interjected Alicia. "Her father must be one of those starving intellectuals. Their children always turn out like this."

But he was too caught up in the conversation. And dazzled.

"You still haven't told me what interpretation is, and why you're against it."

"Because there aren't any sin-omins."

"Does your father let you read just any old book?"

"No."

"Ah, I think that's good."

"Not just one, all of them."

"And do you like to read?"

"No. I like the titles. Reflections in Your Golden Eye."

"Quit spouting nonsense," he said indignantly. "If you don't tell us right now where you want us to take you, we'll go away, and then you'll be left here, all alone."

"The two of you will be all alone," declared the little girl with certainty, standing up. Suddenly they looked at each other in fear.

"If I go away, you'll be alone all night and all day," repeated the child.

Alicia felt uncomfortable.

"We're not trying to make you go away," she assured her, attempting to appease the girl.

"Even if I leave you my cat, you'll be all alone."

"But we really like your company. You can stay with us as long as you like."

"Nights are very long at the resort," commented the little girl, as if it were of no consequence.

"That's true," he said. "That's how it's different from the city."

"There's no one around anywhere," added the child.

"And that's horrible," agreed Alicia.

"Anyway, I could go, and I could leave my cat with you."

"Oh, no, Euuuuyllarre, stay, stay here with us."

"He'll keep you company."

"But you can take care of him better if you stay here with us."

"If the two of you are hungry, I can leave and go buy you some sandwiches."

They both became frightened. They began taking large amounts of food from their bag.

"You see? You see? There's enough food for all three of us."

"For the seven of us, because there's my cat, my other cat, the other cat and the other cat of the other cat."

"There's enough for all seven, Euuuuyllarre," he assured her timidly.

"My cats are used to water and they're in the habit of eating fish."

"They're fantastic, extremely beautiful cats, Euuuuyllarre."

"All right, if that's the way it is, I'll stay with you all night. There are always lonely people on the beach. They get bored, and they don't know what to do."

THE INFLUENCE OF EDGAR A. POE ON THE POETRY OF RAIMUNDO ARIAS

"I was good, I swear," said her father, looking at her steadily. His eyes used to be clear and blue, like a little boy's. But as the years pass, they turn dark. Alicia had noticed that trait in the pupils. There was something in life that made them begin to grow dark; they lost their color of a quiet lake where geese see their own reflection. Still waters trembled, inner currents—from afar, from beyond the horizon, beyond the seas—changed the rhythm and tonality of one's eyes. It happened when children were no longer children, when they grew into men with dark eyes, men without eyes, reflecting nothing, you could not see inside them the way you still could into his eyes. She liked to peer deep into those waters. She saw tombs, aquatic animals, stones, shiny spaces, the calm, disturbing geography of the moon. When he finally ceased to be a child, she would no longer be able to see the sea-horse—suspended in its slow forward motion—in his eyes, or the plant with white flowers and golden stalk. She blew on it, the stalk swayed. Her father closed his eyes.

"You're late," she said in her high, clear voice. "Thirty five minutes and two seconds late. For your punishment, there will be no dessert."

She glanced away from him, so that she would not have to look at those troubled waters.

"But Alicia," he protested, "there was a big crowd out there. A lot of people kept coming against me: there were so many I had a hard time even putting one foot in front of the other. Most of the time I kept one foot down and then, very carefully, in what little space there was, I'd lift the other one up and hold it there. That may sound easy, especially to you, since you didn't have to walk along the avenue this afternoon trying to sell Wonder Soap—three for the price of one—it makes you feel refreshed, but it was very hard, I can tell you. There were times when I got tired of holding my foot up like that. And don't forget how heavy the soap case is either. I tried to take my mind off it and think about other things while I held my foot in mid air, waiting for an opening in the street so I could go on. One time I had the chance, but a man came along right next to me, stretched out his huge, solid foot, and put it down on the tile before I could."

"You should have pushed him away," she scolded. His eyes fell. The soap case was at his side: black, shiny leather with letters that said: "Wonder, Ltd. It makes life worth living."

"It wouldn't have been all that easy," he protested. "He was a huge man, a solid mass of granite, and he was in a hurry, coming along intently, driven by some sort of inner relentlessness. He would have run right over me, the way you crush an ant when you're out walking, paying no attention, not caring. That man and all the rest of them— they were in a hurry to be somewhere; nothing was going to stop them."

They had been in this country for six months, but still they didn't know which direction to run in. He wasn't even sure if they were supposed to run.

"Where were they running to?" Alicia asked out of curiosity.

"I don't know," he confessed. He tried to sneak a cigarette and light it, but she saw him.

"Four," she declared brutally; "you've only got one left."

"I think this makes three," he said, trying to bluff her. "Remember, I shared the one I had this morning with you; besides I was in such a hurry I didn't enjoy it."

"Four," she repeated, still in her chair. In that blue dress, the long hair cascading over her shoulders, she looked remarkably like her mother. Her mother had never owned a blue dress, and she always wore her hair short; the way he saw it, this difference only made the similarity more striking. It might have been her mother's sister she really looked like, but he couldn't be sure; the only time he had ever seen her was when his wife left them. He ran into her by chance at the supermarket; they couldn't talk very long because they were both in a hurry, he had to fix the child something to eat, and write a work about the influence of Edgar A. Poe on the poetry of a very famous author that no one had ever heard of because he had never left his non-European country, and she had to hurry back to a clandestine guerrilla hiding-place that she was a cover for. She seemed like a nice girl to him—he would never forget her red hair, obviously a wig to help conceal her identity—and it occurred to him that he really would have liked her to see the work he was writing: the influence of Edgar A. Poe on the poetry of Raimundo Arias, even though she didn't have time for things like that; she looked at him with an intelligent gaze, an intelligence consumed by passion, according to a line by Raimundo Arias who had never met her but who certainly knew her intuitively, no doubt about that. She thought it a pity that he was a small-bourgeois intellectual (as her sister had informed her before she left him) because he looked so kind and intelligent. No matter, he would never forget the red or blue or green or blonde hair of that girl—I should have gotten to know my wife's sister better, he chided himself, but everyone was in a hurry; they had to get on with the revolution, the meals, the lines for buying milk, bread, flour, rice, garbanzos, oil, kerosene, they had to run when the army came, smashing everything in their way, he needed to take care of the child, the result of a cheap birth control device, and besides he was writing a novel about the revolution, sometimes the novel went ahead of the revolution, sometimes the revolution raced so far ahead that it managed to leave the novel behind, and meanwhile his wife left him, she had outdistanced them both, the novel and the revolution, the child stayed with him, they agreed: it's not a good idea to have a child that small with you when you're mixed up in a revolution; to mislead everyone, they said she had run off to Czechoslovakia with another man. "I should have gotten to know my sister's husband better," she thought, but there was no time, she had to work, to stand in line for milk, bread, flour, garbanzos, oil, kerosene, she had to get on with the revolution, and sometimes a person got tired.

"How many bars of soap did you sell today?" Alicia asked, from her chair. Colored stones and a glass giraffe were spread over the small wooden table in front of her. That was all she had been able to take with her when they fled, when they had to leave their country because he was accused of embracing the Marxist-Leninist faith, and of writing articles that were virtual panegyrics to the guerrilla mob trying to undermine the country and the prestige of its institutions. With great dignity he took his little girl's hand—I'm not just some old object that you can carry around in your arms, she said—he threw a few papers together, some clothing, and they were escorted to the ship under police-guard.

"Why don't we kill him now?" the captain asked. "We can say the same as always: they were killed, trying to escape."

"Nobody's waiting for us," said the child, standing at the ship's gunwale while they docked.

"Daughter," he answered. "I am not a famous soccer-player. You know that well enough."

Alicia looked at her father's spindly legs in the only pair of pants he still owned, and mused that as a daughter she hadn't been very lucky. Her father wasn't a soccer player, a boat-builder, or a famous singer (the only thing she had ever heard him sing was "Pull Down the Wire Fences," completely off-key. She sang "Tremble, Tyrants" much better—a key phrase from the national anthem, banned by the government because of its patently subversive nature), or the owner of a trust, or a movie-star. She would just have to accept it. Children don't choose their parents, although parents usually choose their children, this one, yes, Alicia, not that one, an abortion, unnamed.

"I sold twenty-six, plus the one I gave to an old woman, that's twenty-seven. The truth is, I didn't give it to her; she gave me three oranges in exchange. She was selling oranges, nice, red, La Rioja oranges."

"Twenty-six," reflected the girl. "That's not much for the whole day."

"Don't be so hard on me, child; as far as I can see, the only time people in this country take a bath is on Sunday mornings; besides, you have to think of the competition I have from bath jells, bath salts, powdered soap, skin lotion, soap petals, liquid foam, solid foam and foam solid."

Not only was no one waiting for them in this country—or in any other country, for that matter—but their reception was less than warm. As soon as they arrived, they had to present an enormous number of papers: the father's identification card, the daughter's identification card, the father's passport, daughter's passport, the father's visa, daughter's visa, father's certificate of good conduct, daughter's certificate of good conduct, both baptismal certificates, proof that he was single (how can I possibly show you proof that I'm single if I'm married? All right then, your daughter's. And your marriage certificate), certificate of the father's academic studies, certificate of middle studies, certificate of higher studies, both their vaccination records for small-pox, tetanus, hepatitis, tuberculosis, rabies, poliomyelitis, meningitis, asthma and measles. Very carefully, one by one, the girl held them out to the authorities, yellow and black ones; then the child put them away again, meticulously; her father was completely disorganized. They also asked to see his wife before they would let the child enter the country.

"That's impossible," said the man. "My wife didn't come with us."

"Then the child can't stay here," declared the official.

"Why not?" he asked. "I'm her father. I'll be responsible for her."

"Who says you're this girl's father? The only one who would know that for sure is her mother."

"What about our papers?" he answered. "Doesn't it say so, right there in our papers?"

"Papers are not conclusive proof of paternity," maintained the official. "The only one who can really say whether or not you're this child's father is her mother."

"I am not a child," Alicia answered indignantly. "Potentially," (she had learned this word from a schoolbook) "I'm a woman."

"Her mother will have to come here and swear that this child is the result of her marriage with you," growled the official menacingly. "You might be a criminal, a kidnapper, or a child-molester, and this little girl could be your victim."

"Ask her," he protested.

After a few seconds she said: "This man is my father." Actually it had crossed her mind to deny it, it was the first time that being their daughter had depended on her and not on them; she could have said, for example: "No way. He's an imposter, he's not my father," or something like that, the way it happened in serialized novels or on TV. Then she could choose whoever she wanted for her father, or better yet, she could suddenly be an orphan, but she wasn't sure that would bring her any real happiness. It was very hard to find a proper father in your own country; and in another country, it could be even more problematic. Turning into an orphan only gets to be interesting after you're eighteen, when you can get in to see X-rated movies, when you can buy and sell things using your own name, and pay taxes. A long time before that, at the age of twelve or thirteen, you could have children—obviously a much less important act since a person could do it before he could even open a savings account.

They decided to do a blood test to prove his paternity. It wasn't so bad, after all (even though he fainted, the way he always did when he saw blood. You can't carry out a revolution that way, his wife had told him), because they took them to a very nice clinic and gave them something to eat without making them pay, after they had drawn a quarter of a liter more of blood than they needed from him, the way they always did to foreigners—simply because they were foreigners. She wolfed down her food.

"You're eating my blood," he said, feeling so light-headed after they'd taken his blood that the only thing he could keep down was a cup of coffee with cream. Then she had two helpings of bread, with butter and peach marmalade—that's what they called nectarines in this country. In their country, peaches were called nectarines.

The papers never carried any news about the country they were from, and they took this as an affront.

"I want to know what happened to the four hours they stole from me while we were on the boat," she said as soon as the results of the blood test confirmed that he was the child's father, or that it could be anyone with type A.

After four days aboard ship, the captain's order boomed over the loudspeakers, reminding the passengers to move their watches ahead thirty minutes. The first time, the girl refused to obey the order. Her wristwatch stayed at twelve o'clock while everyone else on board moved the hands on their watches forward, around the circumference of the crystal—a very frivolous way to treat time in Alicia's opinion. He didn't force her; she was an anarchist, she believed in freedom.

"Eat your raspberry ice-cream; who knows when we'll have it again," her father reminded her. Raspberries were blackberries; blackberries were called raspberries in the country they had chosen to come to—because they spoke the same language here. "And remember, child, any kind of personal rebellion is bound to fail," he declared, looking pointedly at the girl's watch as it continued to move with its deliberate rhythm of seconds and minutes. The watch was very pretty, with its blue face and silvery numbers; her mother had given it to her before she left. Because out there, where she was going, time was certain to be measured in other dimensions, and life would be much more intense. Her eyes full of tears, Alicia looked at the blue face on her little watch (as though it were a lake, and the hands were necks of swans floating slowly by) and said:

"No one's going to force me to set it ahead."

When they got off the ship, Alicia's watch was four hours behind.

"I'm not behind time: they are the ones who are ahead," she said, looking up at the two enormous clocks in the plaza.

When she finally gave in—like a turncoat—and set her watch to the time people went by in this part of the world, she began to miss the four hours they had stolen from her on the ship.

"What did they do with my five thousand seven hundred sixty minutes?" she asked her father.

He wasn't prepared to answer that question. In fact, he wasn't prepared to answer any question. For many years now, he had been a child himself. He had lived any way he could, to put it mildly, and he was used to being robbed. They had stolen a lot more from him than four hours, and he hadn't been able to do much of anything to change the order of things. The order of things was the order of the people who owned things, and any sort of personal rebellion was bound to fail. As for his wife, wherever she might be—if she still happened to be somewhere—she had been a child herself for a number of years, she lived any way she could, to put it mildly, and she devoted her life to changing the order of things, but the order of things was very resilient.

"Daughter, when we go back they'll return them to you, if we happen to go back someday. If we go by boat."

She didn't find his answer very comforting. She wasn't interested in long-term paybacks. She felt thoroughly victimized, cheated.

What could they be doing with all those hours they had stored away? She thought about boats filled with stolen hours, boats stealthily crossing the ocean with their secret cargo of time. She envisioned phantom boats filled with men who stood watch over vaults containing stolen time, she imagined traffickers of hours waiting for boats in dirty, dark ports, buying and selling hours. She pictured desperate men who bought little boxes with small amounts of time in them, because these traffickers speculated in bought hours. At some old port a man anxiously watches a boat as it approaches, they lower a blue box from the boat, and he buys half an hour, perhaps less, he buys ten minutes, stolen from unsuspecting passengers on a boat, from people forced to emigrate, like her father and herself, from exiles. A man waits desperately at the port, watching large spots of oil float past, he looks anxiously at the white sides of the boat, at both sides, at the tiny blue box, at a small amount of time, a measure of time that he must have for something, and the captain's voice repeats firmly: "Passengers, please move your watches ahead thirty minutes," and it was no longer twelve o'clock, it was no longer twelve o'clock at night on board the white ship that rolled with the rhythm of the waves, it was not twelve o'clock on a black night, at sea; the passengers, powerless, defeated in other battles, followed the order obediently, they adjusted their watches, and suddenly, in the blink of an eye, at once, it was no longer twelve, but twelve-thirty, thirty minutes had vanished from their lives, had gone to fatten the ship's storeroom, to enrich the traffickers of time.

"Bastardthatgavebirth to ships," she cried out in despair.

Twenty-six bars of soap was no great thing, even though they got by on milk and nuts, "they have plenty of calories," said the father, who had learned about these things in a class he had taken before she was born. In the class on child-care they taught him about food calories, the ten correct answers to give children when they begin to be curious about sex, how to clean and sterilize baby-bottles, and what to do while you wait for the doctor to come, but they never said one word to him about how to make a living, with your children, in a foreign country.

And so he kept his silence, and looked up at the clear sky. It was a common, ordinary clear sky, white in tone, with no significant geographical markings. Alicia sighed, aware of her responsibilities. It wasn't very pleasant, being responsible for a father or mother in difficult times like these. Even if her father wasn't very rebellious, he sometimes tried to make decisions on his own, and when he took action on those decisions, he nearly always failed. Whenever that happened, she didn't criticize him much, because her father was very sensitive and she didn't want to discourage him; she had to help develop his personality, even if it was by means of those disastrous projects of his. She had read a few manuals about adults, and although she didn't agree entirely with Freud (she much preferred his rebellious student, Lacan), she tried to keep her father's neurotic depression in check. She was particularly concerned about her father's sex life: she found it extremely irregular and unstable. But he wouldn't talk about it directly, and he kept putting her off with every excuse he could think of. Sometimes he said he was too tired, there were times when he wasn't interested, and even when they walked down the street together and she kept making pointed remarks about the women they saw, he would put up a stubborn show of indifference. First, he said that his aesthetic sensibility needed to change because the women in this country were very different from the ones in their own; then he insinuated that they didn't use enough soap, finally he began to praise black women, when everyone knew they had gotten rid of blacks in this country many years ago.

Alicia went over to the china tea box (made in France) that sat on the table, and looked through it. There were only a few coins left, all from different countries, with likenesses of different oppressors, almost none of them legal currency. As far as the paper money was concerned, it was from the country they had come from, and no bank would take it because there was no gold behind it. She considered wallpapering part of the room with those blue banknotes, but then decided it would be too provincial. And she was a citizen of the world. Unlike her father.

"We don't have any money," she said flatly. Nearly every day she said the same thing. Then her father would search through the pockets of his only suit for the memorandum book with addresses of his friends and acquaintances, he paged through it meticulously, without success, since most of the people were already dead, weren't at those addresses anymore, or lived thousands of kilometers away. But he liked the routine. When it comes to friends, we're almost always left with useless addresses.

"I don't think we can ask anyone for money today," her father remarked, in that same flat tone.

Alicia sighed and went over to the large hat box that she had stuffed full of clothing before they started on their journey.

"I'll be back in three or four hours, wait for me," she told her father as she was leaving. He watched her go, with a melancholy gaze. She didn't look bad in that Indian costume he had given her once for a school festival. The feathers were a little droopy, and several had been lost on the trip. Alicia had repainted them with watercolors, trying to give them an exotic, picturesque air. There were blue feathers, red, yellow, black and white ones.

"Do you have any idea what kind of feathers the Charrúas wore?" she asked her father. None at all: the Spaniards had killed off all the Indians in that country, and as for a certain descendant who claimed to be 104 years old, he looked about as much like an Afghan as he did an Indian. He wasn't even sure they wore feathers, the way Metro-Goldwyn-Mayer portrayed them.

"I'll put on three more yellow ones; no one will notice the difference," declared Alicia.

She picked up the brushes and began to paint her face, trying to make her expression look terrifying and ugly. Tomato sauce was very effective, but she'd had problems once when a cat, excited by the smell, jumped up on her. He watched her with silent admiration. Her skin was too pale for a real Indian, but Europeans didn't notice those details; at least, the kind of Europeans who were willing to stop on the sidewalk and give a few coins to a little Indian girl.

"Be careful around old men, child, most of them are terrible lechers," her father warned her every time she went out. "Don't let any of them get near you; they like to seduce little girls."

"And it's even worse if they're Indian virgins," finished Alicia, reciting the part of his speech that she knew by heart.

She looked at herself in the mirror. This time she had created a terrifying—and quite satisfying—effect at the height of her mouth. A little shadow around her eyes, false wrinkles, the blue of her eyebrows and a painted-on scar gave her an air of old age that she had seldom achieved.

Looking at herself in the mirror, she said:

"I don't know whether to carry a sign with me that says 'Latin American Indian Girl,' or if I should make one that says 'Old Latin American Dwarf'."

"I'm not sure the Indians had dwarfs," her father remarked.

"Neither am I," she mused. It was incredible how ignorant a person could be about his own ancestors. That didn't happen very often in Europe. The people in Europe were better educated: they could always trace their family tree back five or six generations, they never had revolutions, and nearly all the countries had a parliament. Some had two chambers; others didn't.

There was only one time that she'd had a minor accident when she dressed up as a Latin American Indian girl. It was when a horrible little boy, just slightly younger than herself, came up to her, Machiavellian-like, and yanked on her single Indian braid with all his might; then, forgetting herself and that she was only supposed to mutter unintelligible sounds, she insulted him in perfect Spanish, quickly blaming her bad language on the Spanish colonization of the native civilizations of La Plata. Finally, it all reached a climax when she gave him a solid smack to the jaw that left the entire city sprawled flat on its back.

He looked at her with no little anguish and with real admiration too. She thought something had happened to the genes between generations; some obscure modification of the hereditary traits allowed today's children to be admirable, perfect parents to the people who had given them birth.

This was another race, endowed with a unique resistance, and in the womb they had assimilated the lessons of intimate, highly obscure defeats; in the mother's uterus they had learned sadness, failure, desolation, and when they saw the light of the world they knew how to live, in spite of everything. Conceived in bitter nights, nights of pain, persecution, uncertainty, misery and terror, conceived in houses like jail cells, or in jail cells like tombs, in beds that were coffins, the survivors of those tortured nights of pain were born with a mark of resilience and strength.

Alicia glanced back at him before she left. Her head was full of feathers, and she wore a straw skirt, her very white legs showing underneath. Her chest was bare, revealing the beginnings of round, discreet breasts with tender, rosy points. She carried no bow because her father had never been able to buy her one—he was always short on money. Their gazes crossed, different, different but transparent. They could decipher the signs in each other's eyes. They had learned how to do that during long, sleepless nights on the high seas, when there was no moon to light their way. There, while smoking rationed cigarettes and plotting how to make off with a ham sandwich from the kitchen, they learned to read into the waters of each other's eyes, gentle waters of the father, troubled waters from the lake of the daughter. Alicia looked at him and read, she read the deceptions, the illusions, the sadness.

And when she opened the door and made her voice sound like a little Latin American Indian girl who had fled to Europe, she said to him very clearly:

"I know that what you are thinking about our generation is entirely wrong."

SIMULACRUM

Sergio shook some of the moon dust from his right boot, then sat down and looked around, disappointed. He was all alone, no sign of Patricia anywhere. He had lost her twice today, and night was almost here. He couldn't follow her very closely: she had told him not to, and sometimes he had a hard time finding her again. Then he would feel a little depressed, he'd sit down and wait for time to pass. He would clean his boots, or look down at the bottom of a shallow crater. Sometimes he'd reach into his pocket, pull out an old page written in French or Persian, and try to decipher it. It was slow-going, and the results were hardly encouraging. He knew French much better than he did Persian, but the page he read didn't always bring him pleasure. It might be statistics or an article on economics instead of a poem, but he deciphered them all the same way, at a snail's pace. Or he'd take a little opium, and in the dreamlike state the sedative brought on, he saw the wake of distant cities as they drifted past. He threw little objects into the crater, things that never landed, but floated continually, in an endless spiral. He threw in crumpled wads of paper, pieces of glass, rocks. And messages for Patricia, even if she never picked up those secret invitations, never read them, never answered them. He liked the incessant dance that at one instant made a quartz crystal appear close-up, and then his watchcase, or perhaps Patricia's sweet name engraved on a chunk of metal. No one was allowed to use the craters, and although it was forbidden to throw things in them, something was always dancing around inside, as though they were crystal balls and not craters. Night would come, the long lunar night, and for a long while afterward he would not find that solitude again, moon dust clinging to his boots, empty space, or a circling ship. A landscape with no trees, no vegetation, with fixed colors: the surface always ashen, the air forever dark. The lack of trees made him sad, only because he couldn't leave messages on them for Patricia. Messages that would say: "I waited here for you." "I read a page from *The Idiot*." "The blue agate in this crater is for you." He kept nothing for himself in order to give everything to her, even though he wasn't really sure she appreciated his sacrifice. According to all the data, Patricia was incapable of love. He thought about it often. How could someone who was so loveable also be insensitive to love? His pocket computer confirmed it immediately: Incapable of love--Incapable of love. She didn't seem to feel very comfortable when someone was loving her either. Opening wide her cold, blue eyes—those eyes of stone, of herons, that made him shiver—she saw without understanding, listened without hearing, she caressed without caressing. Being very intelligent, Patricia had learned all the motions and poses of love, kindness, affection, passion, tenderness, and she displayed them perfectly, but they were like a ritual, passages, steps of a traditional dance that revealed nothing within. As he thought about it, Sergio grew troubled once more, and decided not to wait any longer. Was it possible that she didn't know he was waiting for her? She knew. They had made a date on the intercommunicator. His intercommunicator was tuned to Patricia's frequency, but Patricia kept hers tuned to several frequencies, or sometimes to none at all. In fact, he was the one who had made the date with her, as usual.

"Patricia, at five o'clock, in sector DJ7, by the crater."

She had said yes, because even though she was indifferent, she was still polite. Of course she liked to see him, talk with him, eat something chilled or drink something ice cold, perhaps even listen while he read some ancient composition aloud. But it was also possible that in the meantime something would come up and she would forget their date, no, she won't forget it, she'll simply put it off, cancel it on her own, without even trying to locate his frequency to give him an excuse, some sort of explanation. And if she showed up afterward, she still wouldn't be able to understand his uneasiness—his disgust—at all. She would think it very odd when she found him looking so glum.

"I've been waiting for you," he would scold her.

"Why?" she would ask, completely innocent.

"Didn't we have a date?"

"Of course. But on my way over, something came up."

"What?"

"Something. I don't remember now. Anyway, you shouldn't wait for me when I'm late; you ought to know that by now."

"Why don't you look at your memory-meter. If something kept you for four hours, you should know what it was."

"That's what I like most about memory: it has the ability to forget. All I remember now is that something came up—I don't know what—and I couldn't keep our date. And just the way our date slipped my mind when something else came up, now that I've kept the date I can't remember what it was. No, I won't look at my memory. I wouldn't want to live with all those certainties."

Sergio always consulted his memory-meter. He was glad that it kept a record of everything: his every thought, the contours of the landscape, names of seasons, a word overheard by chance. He kept all this material in a file, and sometimes he passed the time pleasantly, projecting it on a screen, so that nothing he had seen, experienced or thought would fall through any crack in his memory.

"You're going to grow old prematurely, you'll be the victim of a memory so full of details," Patricia told him, disdaining his anxieties.

"And you, you'll never know who you really are, who you've been and who you will become."

She laughed rather frivolously.

"Who cares? The woman who was, is gone now, and the woman who is, doesn't care who she'll be."

Although that wasn't the reason it had been invented, Sergio used the memory-meter to reproduce life, alarmed by its swift passing. Perhaps only the immortals could ignore memory, and he wasn't sure that he was immortal. Some people had actually reached the age of 500, but how could anyone know if they were really immortal? A lot of people still died, and even if they didn't die, it could happen anytime; that was something nobody could really be certain about. He thought there was a very good chance that Patricia would be immortal despite the fact that she was only thirty-five years old—she showed signs of it. She had never been sick, nothing seemed to affect her. She was in perfect health, and she was extraordinarily adaptable. Sergio shuddered as he thought of the years to come, when she would still be alive and he would be dead. She was able to do so many things, he felt sure that Patricia's life would be full of variety, would be multifaceted. He, on the other hand, suffered from many different things. Moon dust, for example, hurt his lungs. He didn't feel very good when there was a dramatic change in the temperature either, the way it happened when they went from one atmosphere into another, and Patricia was always so amused when she found him freezing cold, outside his ship, trying to make all the temperature controls work. The food they had there didn't agree with him either: he had been hospitalized more than once when his body couldn't adapt.

In the machine-room his boss told him, "You ought to ask for a transfer—for your health." He didn't answer: he had waited so long, and gone through so much bureaucratic red tape, to get this position, close to Patricia, that his boss's advice sounded absurd. He thanked him anyway. His mother was concerned about his health too. Almost every Sunday (if Patricia was busy making love or taking part in some sports event) he went to visit his mother. The trip took him far away; he liked to get in his vehicle and start out on that long, lonely journey through space. There was very little traffic on the way because the route was so far from everything, and besides that, it wasn't a workday. Sometimes, way off in the distance, he would pass another vehicle, and it would greet him by sounding its sirens and turning on its lights. Inside his cabin he couldn't hear the sirens, but he could see the lights. Still, his instruments picked up the sound of the other engine. He would turn on all his instruments except the automatic pilot: he liked flying his vehicle through that solitude. He especially liked the colors of things that had very light hues. Every time he thought he had grown used to the new colors, he would check his memory-meter to remember how he felt when he first began to travel in space. His cabin was very comfortable, and he kept it neat and clean. Whenever he could, he would put in something that wasn't mechanical, to make it feel cozier. He hung up prints of flowers, painted the seats in soft colors, decorated the canned goods. It was the most secluded place he knew, since they hadn't assigned him to any living quarters in particular—and it would be a long time before that would happen. About the only thing they were constructing these days were buildings for research or work, control centers, stations, health centers. And the workers went back to their own homes, through space, to inhabited planets, or they stayed in the buildings and used the halls as improvised dormitories. He stayed there because Patricia never went anywhere. She didn't sleep either, and her insomnia was one of the things that truly bothered him, because then he couldn't follow her. And yet, the specialists had found nothing abnormal in Patricia's insomnia: only a strange, mysterious something in the genes, a dark, perverse seed, an intruder in her garden that transformed long nights into long trips, voyages through endless, empty space, a nocturnal journey to different cities, her nights were unexplored territory, an appointment with a time and space that he knew nothing about.

His mother watered the garden while she waited for him. He landed some distance away and took a helicopter to her house. He loved his mother and the way she could adapt. She didn't want to be isolated, confined to a hospital, or shut up in one of those old cities they kept as museums: she demanded a role, she wanted to be able to participate, to have a place in the process. The Brigade Commander gave her a suitable job in a specially aerated green-house: preserving rare species, unique trees, plants that were in danger of becoming extinct, the sole examples and witnesses of a world in decline. Two or three workers helping his mother rounded out the personnel, and she lived very comfortably, completely devoted to the care of those plants. Every evening she went back to her nice, new home, a building where most of the staff assigned to the Department of Flora Conservation lived. But they also let her use a little plot of land for her own garden, and there his mother grew begonias, dahlias, hydrangea, not forgetting the roses, her son's favorite flowers. His mother had adapted very well to her new way of life, and she often reflected with her son:

"These last few years (she meant as long as she had worked for the Department of Flora Conservation) have been the most beautiful time in my life. Not only have I seen poverty, injustice, hunger, pain and cruelty disappear, but at an age when I could only wait for death and be a burden to the State, my son and my neighbors, I've found that my body and my mind can still be very useful to society."

Sergio watched her becoming healthier every day, and deep down he admired her. Although she had once grown old very quickly, ever since the new order of things had taken over she had stopped ageing. From that time on she had experienced no illness or disturbance of any sort, and had maintained a delicate balance of contemplation and activity. She liked looking at old pictures, and as soon as the film stopped she would remark to her son:

"That was a terrible time. There was still private property, and the powerful accumulated things and prospered at the expense of the hunger and pain of the common people. It was a time when one man's wealth was so great that he could buy up an entire country. Many perished who could have lived in other circumstances, and many others died before they could be born."

These thoughts troubled Sergio. He asked himself how it was possible to live in a world like that, filled with pain, injustice, wars, exploitation, contempt, competition, blackmail, repression, speculation, fraud, lies, robbery, panic, child rape, violence, distrust, fear, alienation, frenzy, catastrophe. Fortunately, that had all disappeared before he was born, and there was no sign that it would ever return.

Sergio grew tired of waiting and, dejected, he looked down at the bottom of the crater where a few pieces of glass he had thrown in were doing a slow, endless dance. Mentally, he offered them to Patricia. "If you could come," he thought, "if you would like to come, I would tell you that the quartz is a tiny house a person can live in, the red one is a flint, and that celestial child jumping rope is a rock crystal I found at the beach during one of my trips, I bent down, thinking of you, and I picked it up so that you would always know I offer you the universe, with its smallest objects." His mental speech disturbed him. Patricia didn't like that sort of message.

"That woman," his mother said to him on Sunday, while they were talking in her tiny home, "are you sure she loves you?"

"No. She doesn't love me, Mother," he answered, trying to keep his voice from breaking. His mother looked at him sadly.

"Couldn't you...?" she began to say without conviction.

"What would be the point of my loving someone who would love me back?" he interrupted, not letting her continue. "That would only be a pleasant exchange. I think the real reason I love her is because she doesn't love me, and she never will, even though I love her so much. I feel that the fact that I love her when she doesn't return my love is the most definitive proof I can offer of how much I love her," he concluded.

"As long as it doesn't lead you down the road to sorrow or despair," his mother seemed to advise him.

"Poor Mama," he thought. "Am I not even a little bit transparent, then?"

He got into his vehicle and moved it forward. Slowly. Because he had already waited a long time and now he didn't know what to do. He decided to take a spin through space, fly in orbits, approach quiet, well-lighted cities. From a distance, the city lights made him feel good, beneficent. As though many mothers were waiting for him to come home. Off in the distance, the cities looked inoffensive, offering shelter. Only the lights were visible, and they accompanied anyone venturing out into the soothing peacefulness of space.

He went around several times, made a few bold incursions (when he was sad he liked to turn cartwheels in the air, like an acrobat), then slid in slowly, brushing the calcareous surface of the moon. On his last run he saw Patricia's vehicle parked not far away. Patricia seldom used it, because the moon was her permanent home. Nothing could take her from there. She turned down trips, passages, excursions that would take her away. She never felt homesick, she never left anything behind that could bring her back to the same place someday, that would remove the pain from her heart.

Still, he was glad to see Patricia's craft; it meant she wasn't far away. Night was coming on—his watch said so—with no change in light or atmosphere, but while all activity came to a halt and everyone went back to their place of rest, the longest and least explored time of day was just beginning for Patricia: the night of insomnia. He didn't go out looking for her, because he thought that might bother her. He made a few passes around Patricia's vehicle, as though paying her homage, as if they—those passes—were the steps of a nuptial dance.

He saw her appear—covered with ashes—gaily straightening her clothing. She had on her metal garments, and Sergio watched her place the breastplates over the slight elevation of her white breasts. He remained quietly in his ship, parked a short distance from Patricia's. A man emerged next to her, climbing up from the bottom of a ravine where they had taken shelter, he left her and walked away, waving goodbye. He wondered who the chosen one was this time—while she had left him for later. But the man saw Sergio in his ship, and even though he didn't know him, he waved anyway. Patricia looked happy, playful; Sergio moved his ship forward a few meters to meet her. He held out his hand and helped her climb in. As usual, he was startled by the extreme coldness of her touch.

"Hello," Patricia greeted him. She was still arranging her dress. He would have preferred seeing her naked, but he had to admit that it was rather chilly.

"Hello," answered Sergio after he had helped her in. "Do you want something to drink?"

"I'll take some coffee," she said, still aroused. "Is it nighttime already?"

He looked at the dials on the panel.

"It's been night for exactly an hour and ten minutes."

"That's good!" said Patricia, settling into the seat next to the steering wheel.

He served her cold coffee. Patricia detested hot drinks.

"Do you want to go for a ride?" Sergio asked while sipping his own steaming coffee. He tried to hide his disappointment. Sometimes Patricia would agree to a short flight around the moon, not too far, not going near sleepy city lights that made her sad.

"No," she answered. "I'd rather you read me one of those old writings. A poem, if you don't mind."

This was Sergio's sensitive point. Drawn to the secret enchantment of old writings, he spent all his free time reading and translating them. He specialized in dead languages, and although his specialty was of hardly any practical use at all, he took great pleasure in the never

46

ending task of digging into the past, searching for their traces, their signs, their testimonies. Their fading light. Patricia always listened to him carefully. He didn't know what she really felt—if she felt anything—from those melancholy writings, but there was this: she listened to them in silence, raising the cold goblet to her mouth, sometimes pouting her lips until they came into contact with the hard glass. The tip of her tongue appeared, voluptuous, between her lips; she touched it softly against the glass, again and again, and he shivered, imagining what pleasures its contact could bring. She seemed unaware of her facial expressions. Of the secret, reddish tongue that appeared like a small snake between her lips and pressed repeatedly against the glass.

"I didn't bring any poems today," he said, resentment showing in his voice.

"Oh, dear," she said sweetly. "Our Sergio sounds angry. He's offended." She reached out her white arm to Sergio's blond hair. "Well then, tell me about the old poets. The way they stammered. Their apprenticeship, their decline. Be good. Pretty Sergio has gotten angry," she said, still touching his hair.

He brushed away her caress, softly. He wished he could be one of those strong guys Patricia made love with. She always chose dark men, athletic, rather coarse and clumsy, with no imagination. He knew exactly what sort of people she would pick for her love sessions. Just so she could lie naked. So she could amuse herself, make love as though it were only a meaningless game. He wasn't like that at all. There was something delicate in his body that Patricia didn't like, something vulnerable that she didn't want to wound, even though she was constantly wounding him.

Sergio reached back into his memory and began to recite a long poem of the troubadours. He wasn't sure of all the words, but in the calm of night, alone in space, with no noise to break the unmerciful silence of the moon, he felt inspired, his imagination filled in the gaps. As he went on, he saw Patricia turning sad; her lips seemed to press tightly against the glass goblet, and when he had finished, she stood up forcefully, and violently pushed him away.

"Why are you always reciting such sad pieces? I hate melancholy and failure. It's not healthy to be sad," she said emphatically.

"It isn't my fault," Sergio defended himself. "I didn't write those words."

"No, but you chose them," she said, looking at him impatiently. "I think you're just trying to hurt me with your recitations. But you can't, my friend: that only lasts a minute. Now then, if you don't mind, let's take a look at a party," she said suddenly, changing the subject and the expression on her face.

Sergio gave in with resignation. Patricia honestly liked parties and social gatherings. Especially at night when she couldn't sleep, when solitude was a fearful enemy she didn't fight, but one that she would rather run from. Faced with solitude or fear of night, Patricia would hook up the projector and watch films of her latest parties. She was a well-known hostess. There, among a crowd of people, surrounded by companions who admired her but did not love her, by suitors who bedded her down with little or no effort, Patricia displayed the full measure of her happiness, her liveliness, all of her energy. Now Sergio saw her on the ship's tiny screen, dancing to the rhythm of various kinds of music, pouring great quantities of alcohol into the fountains, competing in parlor games or sports, taking off her clothes in the middle of a frenzied dance, making love in public to the applause and cheers of the onlookers. When she had finished, breathless and happy, she sat down at the edge of a fountain to talk to her friends and to sip frozen drinks. To Patricia, the only thing that differentiated one man from another was his capacity for pleasure. Hers seemed to be unlimited, even though it was usually only superficial. She found pleasure in being alone or with a companion, naked or dressed, working or idle, she took pleasure in bathing, running, laughing, walking, talking, traveling, being still or moving, she enjoyed every moment of her existence, and she apparently based all her decisions on that singular pursuit: pleasure. She wasn't terribly demanding. The more conditions placed on pleasure, the fewer opportunities there are to have it. The only horror was death, and for Patricia, pleasure was the opposite of death. The fear of losing pleasure was next to death.

Sergio watched her as the film was showing. He could see her in the dark. What was there about her that he didn't know? His love was like a mother's: all-encompassing: it held the past, however it had been, the present, the way it was, the future, no matter how it would turn out. "Incapable of loving," said the computer. "In love with Patricia," the machine answered every time he asked it about his own feelings.

When the film was over, Patricia was aroused. The memory of the party had excited her again.

"I want to make love," she announced. She looked around the ship, as though searching for some object or some thing she could use. Finally, her eyes rested on him.

Sergio shuddered, and in his discomfort he couldn't tell if Patricia's declaration filled him with resentment or wonder.

"Yes. Why are you so surprised? I've just made love, but now I want to do it again. It's nighttime now. Sometimes it feels very long to me. Everyone is sleeping. Everyone in the world is asleep. I don't want to feel alone. No, the truth is, I don't want to *be* alone. You ought to be asleep yourself, right now. Do you think it's insomnia that's creating this anxiety in me, this voraciousness? Oh! I could make love all night long! Are you tired?"

"No," answered Sergio.

She laughed.

"You poor fellow," she added. "You're just saying no to be agreeable. I made you wait for hours, you saw me coming out of the ravine with another man, and yet you tell me you're not tired. You could even make love with me right now, just to please me."

"To please me," corrected Sergio.

"Wrong," said Patricia. "You're looking for something else. I wouldn't please you; you're afraid of being next to me. No, you're not looking for pure, simple, meaningless pleasure—inconsequential—touching the skin, oh the dark skin that covers another person's body. Only the skin. Wandering over that tense, pulsating surface. Nothing more. Caressing and licking. Inhaling and touching. Touching and pressing. Pressing and sucking. Sucking and inhaling. Inhaling and even more, much more, sinking in, penetrating, breaking, subjugating. You wouldn't be able to keep still. You'd have to express something besides the primitive sensation of acknowledgement: I and the other. The other and I. I know I'm with another because I touch him. I feel him. I recognize him with my fingers, my tongue, my hips and my teeth. It's the only way I can be certain of him. I know that I'm with another because he touches me, he feels me, recognizes me with his fingers, his tongue, his hips and his teeth. Don't you see the beauty of it? That way you know you're with someone else. I couldn't do that with you. You would inhibit me. You'd make me think. You aren't that sort of happy animal. Your animality is complicated. My animal side is stripped down, bare. My animal side is a free animal: it has no feelings. An animal without pretensions. It eats and fornicates, fornicates and works, works and sings, sings and eats, eats and laughs, laughs and searches for basic things."

"What is she afraid of?" wondered Sergio. That woman was afraid of something. He wasn't going to have a metaphysical discussion with her—or any other kind of discussion either.

"I'm someone else, and you don't feel me, you don't touch me, you don't recognize me with your teeth," argued Sergio, unenthusiastically. She was aroused now, revealing her naked body to him, and at this moment he had no desire to argue. What he really wanted to do was leave. Go far away, or lie down with her. Everything other than leaving or lying down felt sterile to him, unconstructive.

"I hear you, I see you and you're alive, I argue with you, I understand you, I admire you, you trouble me, worry me, you make me want to rebel as an act of metaphoric, misplaced love. That's why I can't have sex with you. It would be almost like loving you."

Sergio quickly stood up, he jumped to the ground, closing the ship's door behind him, leaving her inside. It was his ship, but he was going to abandon her anyway. He had never left her like this before, but now he felt irritated, impatient.

He didn't turn his head, but he could imagine her laughter as she saw him going.

It was late, and no other vehicles were on the road. He turned on his communicator and spoke to the station chief.

"I'm far away, and I'm lost," he told him.

"Ah ha," answered the chief.

"I'd like to go back home, see people. Human faces, friends, what can I tell you, do you have some sort of work I can do that's out of the ordinary?"

"You sound a little nervous to me, son. Take your pulse and watch your blood pressure. You need to take care of yourself."

"Quit giving me advice. I'm asking for help. Is there any girl who's free tonight, who would like to sleep with me?"

"Come on, Sergio. What are you saying? Everyone has gone home. Besides, I don't know what kind of girl you're talking about. Have you been watching an old movie?"

"Yes, chief. I watch the same movie every day."

"I'll send a ship for you. Tell me your exact location. But do me a favor: Calm down, and don't move. Give yourself an injection or something. And stop bringing me headaches."

He didn't give himself an injection, but he was too agitated to stay in the same place. Besides, he was cold. He was always cold on the moon at this time of night. He had left the air temperature machine inside his ship, and now he was shivering. It was damned cold there, and he had no way to fight it. He was going to suggest that they put individual temperature machines along the road. Next to the craters or somewhere. They still needed to make a lot of changes.

Someone was calling him on the intercommunicator. He tuned it in, hoping it would be Patricia.

"Are you still alive?" he heard his chief drawl. "Don't move. I've already sent a ship out to find you."

"I'm cold," complained Sergio.

The chief swore at him and shut down the transmission.

He saw the ship coming, and felt happy. He wanted to go home, or anywhere. Before climbing in, he took out a chisel and wrote on a rock crystal: "Patricia, I love you." He threw it in the nearest crater and watched it dance around.

"People are always throwing crap in the craters," complained the driver, disgruntled because the mission had gotten him out of bed.

AFTERNOON OF THE DINOSAUR

He went down to the beach, lugging all his gear. Duck feet, wetsuit, tripod, fishing net. Before going out, he knocked at his parents' bedroom door, but there was no answer. They were probably asleep. Or maybe they were dead: that might be why they didn't answer. He thought about this possibility for a second, but then decided that even if they were dead, he would go down to the beach anyway. It was a grey afternoon, a few slow, heavy, lavender clouds slid across the sky like old, dignified, marble matrons; the sea, calm, tight, nearly solid, gave hints of vague inner swells; it was the sort of afternoon the dinosaur would pick to come out of the water and show himself on the beach. And if his parents really were dead, he would take care of that later. Or someone else could do it for him. Taking the steps to the street two at a time, he tried to imagine what would have to be done if his parents were dead. That was something they hadn't taught him at school. In school all they ever taught was useless things, like very complicated equations, when it was common knowledge that machines could do all those things now. Even in underdeveloped, backward countries like his, machines could do everything. His father took him to his office once. Not his first father, the second one. This one. He had a whole office, all to himself. It wasn't like he was just some ordinary employee, but as if he was a boss or something. He gave orders on the Dictaphone, and showed him around the office as though it was all his, as if he, all by himself, with some enormous effort, had placed stone upon stone, brick upon brick, and between stone and brick, the requisite lime and mortar. He was probably just some high-ranking employee, he had already seen how people like that acted, if they were high-ranking employees (and sometimes even the ones who had to settle for giving orders to a simple gate-keeper) they acted like the whole company belonged to them, as though all the other employees were their servants, their subjects or vassals. They had no sense of class.

"Their problem is they don't have any sense of class," his father told him. The first one. The one he didn't have anymore, the one who didn't give him presents of underwater diving gear.

"Do you have a cigarette?" his father had asked him, the first one, the one who didn't have an office, a house in the city, or another one on the beach or one in the mountains either, or his own car, he didn't have a TV set or a refrigerator or leather moccasins or cigarettes or anything. He searched his pockets, and crammed in with the things he pulled out was a thoroughly mashed cigarette. His father immediately stuck it in his mouth, without even bothering to glance at the label.

"It's English," he told him.

"Is it?" said his first father, indifferently. "So then— how do you like English tobacco?"

"It smells too strong," he answered, trying to be noncommittal. He stole cigarettes from the father he had now. He was always leaving half empty packs in the pockets of every jacket he owned.

They came to the park; the air felt chilly.

"If you want me to, I'll get you an overcoat," the boy offered his father number one. He thought he must be cold, wearing only that light beige suit. Besides, the color didn't go with the season. Underneath the suit, his shirt was worn and threadbare. He imagined how his mother would hit the roof if she could see him dressed like this. His mother. That is, his father's wife, who wasn't his wife anymore, even though she was still his mother. Why couldn't you divorce your mother, the way his father had? He was going to get him an overcoat, not because of what his mother might say, but for his own sake—he must be freezing. With two fathers, his life was always busy.

His father number one smiled, and said softly:

"How would you get it?"

He made a vague gesture. He didn't like giving away his secrets.

In father number two's office everything was polished and in its proper place. His father had only invited him, he hadn't invited his sister: apparently he thought women didn't belong in offices. He had a lot of ideas like that. He was very authoritarian. And he didn't offer many explanations. Not like his father number one who was much kinder and softer, and always explained everything. He thought his father used the explanations for himself, because his life was so hard. Especially after the war. Because there had been a war—just a little war, not a big international war, a local war, an internal one, a war inside the country's borders, but a war just the same. Nobody wanted to talk about it, and it wasn't in any book you could find, and apparently his father number one had a hard time getting through it.

"That man is an intellectual," his second father said once, with contempt. The war had given some people a sense of security, while it brought others a feeling of insecurity, and a lot of things seemed different. It was hard to know what they'd been like before.

"Are you an intellectual?" he asked his father number one.

"No," he answered. "I'm a journalist. That's someone who's paid to write things he doesn't think, in newspapers financed by private industry, so that he'll say whatever they want him to. In other words, a worker with a pen," he said sardonically. "A slave."

"Why don't the companies say those things?"

"They don't like to attract attention to themselves. They'd rather pay someone to say what they want people to believe. It's all very complicated, my boy."

He had never seen his father's name after any newspaper article.

"Don't you want to attract attention either?" he asked him.

"Well, first of all, it doesn't seem right for me to put my name on things I don't agree with, and second, the corporations would rather have things come out without a by-line. As if everyone held that same opinion, the one common sense and history tell us is right."

He didn't like the situation. He liked it better when his father wasn't working. Although, come to think of it, that didn't seem to have been a particularly good time for the rest of the family. The rest of the family was his mother because, as far as his sister was concerned, she was too small back then to have any memories. And his second father hadn't come into the picture yet. One day when his father was in the mood to talk, he showed the boy nearly all the articles he had written. They were scattered around the room at his rooming house, tucked in among packets of tea leaves, empty cigarette cartons, bottles of grappa and assorted socks with no mates. His father had always been disorganized, and the less space he had to work in, the more efficiently he could disorganize things. The articles were fascinating, and they both enjoyed sorting through them and reading them. Some were slightly singed by the fire from the primus, or from the little stove he had for keeping himself warm in winter, or by a cigarette. Mice and cockroaches had nibbled on others. In the pile, he found articles about cultivating roses, the best weather for sailing, how to make a delicious rice cake, and the importance of always having a smile on your face. You could see that his father was a very clever man. He could write anything. He had never planted a rosebush in his life, he was deathly afraid of sailing, and he was positive that the recipe for rice cake was sheer invention, since his father hated rice.

His father number two ordered him to come along to the office. He never invited anyone; he gave orders, apparently certain that his orders fit in perfectly with everyone else's wishes. He woke him early, going into his room without knocking, and informed him with great satisfaction:

"You're coming to the office with me today."

He didn't blink, he started dressing because he didn't like to argue. He was sure his new father thought it was the one thing he secretly wanted more than anything else in the world. On his way to the bathroom, he passed by his sister's room. After they had moved in with this father, they each got their own room. It was more comfortable, but it took longer when one of them felt an urgent need to talk to the other.

He found his six-year old sister looking philosophically through a comic book while scratching her toes.

He went in without knocking, and she raised her eyes from the magazine, impassively.

"The old man wants me to go to the office with him," he announced.

"Where is Chad?" she asked, not responding.

"In Africa, I think," he answered.

"Are the good guys the government or the Communists?" she asked again.

"I don't know," he said. "It all depends. What are you reading?"

"A comic book. The main character lives in Chad. I can't tell if she's working for the CIA or if she's a Red subversive."

"I'll ask our father number one," he said. "Well, this time I'm glad you're a woman. You won't have to go to the office."

He left, and continued on to the bathroom. When he came out again, his father was waiting impatiently, car keys in his hand. His father number one had never owned a car. He managed to get hold of a bicycle once, but when he left it unchained it was stolen.

His father's office was full of furniture and equipment. He gave a few orders into the Dictaphone and sat down in the armchair as though that entire world of objects and machinery all belonged to him. It was a movable armchair, and he swung back and forth on it, his legs spread wide. He turned back and forth in satisfaction. His shoes shone, like the furniture, like the floors. It occurred to him that if he had brought his small camera (a present from his father number two on his last birthday; his father number one always gave him more original, less ambitious things: a box of matches from Teruel, a war stamp from Spain, or simply nothing), he would have been able to take a striking photograph, an enormously effective photo. Under the shiny boots of his father number two, below the fine, perfectly ironed pants, between the swinging of his rather flabby legs, beneath the portraits of President Vitalicio and the Prime Minister, he could have placed this inscription: "Portrait of a Man of Success." Success being a small town in the North, with gleaming gas stations, lakes with swans and geese, stainless steel picture frames, any number of banks where you could open an account without sitting down, full of the satisfactions-a-person-toils-for-all-his-life. All the survivors of the war meet in Success, just to celebrate the fact that they're still alive. The ones who lost the war never meet, first of all because they're either dead or they're in prison, and secondly because no one would ever let them in. His father number one liked to tell him stories about the citizens of Success. He knew them all by sight, for one reason or another. He didn't have a passport to Success, but that didn't seem to bother him much.

"My son," his father declared in a priestly manner, and the ceremonious tone jolted him out of his daydream. "Bang!" he thought. "You are transcendental. It's because I don't eat." That's the way all his speeches started. In that same tone, and with the word "son." It made him shiver to hear himself called that. He'd had nothing to do with it. He hadn't asked anyone to bring him into the world, they hadn't let him choose the year, the era or the country, they hadn't given him permission to make a detailed study of the constitutions and histories of the different places in the world before they dropped him violently into this one. On the other hand, he didn't have a lot of confidence in the truthfulness of history, the history we know is always the history that's told by the winners. Why don't we know the history of the others, huh? huh?

"My son," repeated the father. What was he going to ask him, huh? On the floor was a tiny dust ball, all by itself. Slowly, he inched his foot toward it. When next to it, he kicked it, hard.

"My son," his father said again. At this rate, with one word coming along every five minutes, he was sure to miss school, and he would miss the movies after school too. He went to school so that he could go to the movies—they were his true passion. He liked all the movies, every single one of them. What he liked most of all was the atmosphere inside the theaters. The lights turned down low, a faint crinkle of caramel candy wrappers when nervous hands began to untwist the paper, smothered laughter, a warm, humid breath that seemed to emanate from the screen, he even liked the fleas he was always picking up at the movies, and that he took home enthusiastically, to the despair of his number one and only mother. Today they were showing "Darker than Amber" and "The Secret Life of Napoleon." He had already seen about six or seven lives of Napoleon, every one of them different. He was also familiar with the private lives of Helen of Troy, Cleopatra, Sampson and Delilah, Solomon, the four pharaohs, Louis XV, Henry VI, Richard III, and Carlos Gardel. The further back the character was in history, the more details they showed about his life—he didn't know why. On the other hand, he had seen only one movie about Che Guevara—a very bad one—and none about Fidel Castro. That's the way it was with movies.

"This is the latest model of calculator that we've received," his father number two finally announced in a professional tone and with unconcealed pride. "A marvelous machine," he declared. "It can perform any kind of operation in less than a second. It adds, subtracts, multiplies, divides, calculates interest, deducts taxes ('it does embroidery, and even knows how to darn,' he thought, but didn't have the courage to say it out loud), it carries out complex operations, conjugates verbs in three languages, tells you exactly what day the 8th of December will fall on in the year 2345, and it answers simple questions like: What time is it in Japan at this very moment, the latitude of Ireland, the chemical symbol for uranium, the geographical irregularities of Tabago, and what time of year—depending on the country—to plant poplar and cedar trees." He paused as though waiting for the machine's powers to make a deep impression on his audience. Stealthily, he used the pause to scratch his elbow against the wall. And also to think about what the devil he could put in the composition he had to write: "My Future." At school he had a reputation for always coming up with the right answer in math. But he failed at writing essays because the themes were always so perverse: "Memories of My Childhood," "A Morning in the Countryside," "My Parents," "My Country," "My Best Friend," things like that.

"Have you any idea how much one of these machines costs?" his father number two asked. Silence spread like an ill wind. He felt nervous, but thought he should give some sort of answer. Any answer at all. He had to write the composition: "My Future." How much did the machine cost? What was he going to put in the essay?

"I think about 500 thousand 820 futures," he answered quickly.

He was sure his father was only waiting for a chance to tell him how much the machine really cost.

"Millions, my boy, millions!" he corrected the child.

"Anyway, I don't plan to buy that future or any other kind of future," replied the child who was beginning to feel tormented by all the zeros on the right (the ones on the left weren't worth anything as usual, they were there for some reason) and by an equal number of little futures distilled in writing.

"Come here, my boy," his father again assumed the protective, doctoral air that he despised. An air his father number one never used, he must not have the necessary zeros to the right for it, or the future either. "Come here and ask the machine a question—carefully."

He stood before it, obviously feeling very inferior. To begin with, it was a lot bigger than he was. Secondly, it cost more, and in the third place, it didn't seem to have any parents. He had a notion to ask it what he should put in the essay he had to write, but the machine wasn't programmed for that. He looked at his father who was waiting—with obvious pleasure—for his son to ask the machine a question so that it would answer, and after it had answered, to be profoundly impressed, as though he was the one who had invented it, or something like that. He thought: "He seems to be prouder of this machine than he is of me." He asked what the weather was like in Japan at that exact moment, and he was very pleased when the machine answered that it was spring, and the temperature was twenty degrees in the shade with very little humidity, winds blowing at 15 kilometers an hour. He thought that somewhere in Japan the trees must be full of flowers, and the streets and the avenues, that the warm sun was licking at plants and the rooftops of houses, and there was no way he could write about his future. He would have to talk to his father number one about it. The worst disaster had come along that winter when the theme was: "My Parents." He couldn't decide which father to write about, so he wrote about both of them. He tried to be as objective as he could. The teacher didn't like something he had written, and she took him aside.

"My boy, do you know how many sacrifices we had to make so that we could buy this machine?"

"In the first place, you never mention your mother in your composition at all," the teacher reprimanded him.

"Many, my boy, many," emphasized his father number two. "Industrialized countries make them—like the United States, Germany, Japan and France. We have to sell an enormous amount of wool and meat to get just one."

"I thought it only meant men," he defended himself. "That's the problem with plurals that include both sexes. The title was: 'My Parents.' A mother in the singular, combined with a father in the singular, changes into two parents, three parents, or many more. Language is imperialistic," he said.

The teacher was offended by the notion.

"Don't you think you ought to learn a little more before you start handing out opinions about language?"

He did not think so. If he had to wait until he learned everything he didn't know, he'd never be able to judge anything or anyone. Besides he wasn't the one meddling with language: it was language that was meddling with him. Before he could even reason, language had begun to meddle with him, imposing its laws on him, forcing him to give certain names to things, making him believe that those were the only names possible, when later on he would find out that there were other languages, but that his own, the one he had stammered as a child, was useless: North Americans didn't speak it, nor did the Germans, Japanese, Russians or Chinese, and because they made machines like this they were masters of the world.

"One day," continued his father number two, "machines will be able to solve mankind's most difficult problems and questions, and life here on earth will be more comfortable, simpler, uncomplicated."

All right. But who will own the machines, huh? Who owned this one, for instance? His father? The company? Society? Only a certain part of society, or society as a whole? Did his father number one own a tiny part of this machine too? Was he an owner of one of the little buttons, maybe, just one? How would the little machine be divided up? According to a man's status? His stock in the company? The number of children he had?

"That's why," declared his father number two, "we need to plan and organize our future."

What future was his dad talking about? Was it the same as the one in the essay? Anyway, since it sounded like a very important, very rhetorical phrase, he memorized it so he could include it in his essay. "We need to plan and organize our future."

"I'd like to have a talk with your father," the teacher told him. He understood language well enough to know that beneath this gentle suggestion, there was an order. The teacher *wanted* to talk to his father, and it was best to humor her. Why did people say certain things one way, when they really meant something else? That's what he liked too, he liked talking with his own father a lot, with number one, not number two.

"Some day," continued his father, "some day you and I will work side by side, carving out the future with machines like this, even though there's a great difference in our ages."

He would use that bit about 'carving out the future' in his essay too. He never thought that his father would give him so many ideas for his homework. The morning hadn't been a waste after all, at least not entirely.

"And now, my son," concluded his father, "I want you to name this beautiful machine, the symbol of the future, the symbol of family unity, the symbol of man's work and genius. Give it any name you like, and when you're older and the country has many more of these, you'll remember that you were the one who gave them their name."

They were always asking him to do complicated things. Write about the future, name one of these machines. Why couldn't they just leave him alone?

First he went to the rooming house, but his father wasn't there, as usual. The poor little room depressed him with its thin, partition-wall that really didn't separate him from anything, not from the cries of the prostitutes, or the moans of sick people, or drunken laughter, not even from his own thoughts. Then he started looking in all the nearby bars where he was sure to be, his father didn't usually go very far. He hated public transportation: subways, automobiles, buses, bicycles; elevators set him on edge; he preferred to walk.

He tried to think of likely names, names solid and compact like the future, commanding names, names that would fit an organized, orderly future, the machine was like a soldier, rigid and full of metal parts, well-disciplined: a soldier who simply carried out orders, not arguing, unthinking; a soldier, like all of them, built to obey instructions, the plans of those who gave the orders, a soldier free of thought, but indoctrinated, programmed, useful for serving and keeping silent. Would "Obedience" be a good name?

His father didn't seem to care much for his choice, but he decided to stand firm.

"And in the name of the future," he said, "in the name of things to come, order, planning and respect, I name you Obedience." The ceremony was over, although he wasn't one hundred percent sure his father really liked his choice. That's the way things were. You couldn't spend your entire life trying to please everyone.

He went out looking for his father number one in the bars and local bowling alleys. On the corner next to the rooming house was one with a metal counter, hardly any seats, a wooden floor and an old Victrola that kept playing Carlos Gardel's rendition of the tango "Rancor," over and over again. The tango gave him an indefinable, unsettling sensation, that's why his father liked it, and that's why he wasn't really sure he liked it. He found him leaning on the counter, drinking grappa, and holding a very animated conversation with an ugly-looking woman. The bad thing about his father number one was that you could always tell when he was trying to get in someone's good graces. His father didn't see him, so he moved closer, and when he was at his side he said discreetly:

"Dad."

He turned around, startled.

He hadn't been expecting his son right then.

"So this is your little puppy," said the ugly woman, dying with laughter.

He felt put-upon. He didn't know what the ugly-looking woman was laughing at.

"I'm a Newfoundland dog," he said with great dignity.

"A cocker," continued his father, who had recovered from his surprise.

"A Swiss sheepdog," added the child.

"A boxer."

"A German shepherd."

"A bulldog."

"A greyhound."

"A mastiff."

"A bloodhound."

"A Spanish Alano."

"A Pekinese. Dad, can we talk for a minute?"

The woman took a quick sip from his father's glass, and this familiarity bothered the boy.

"I don't like people mocking me to my face," said the woman when she thought their list had run out. She was offended by their collusion, and his father felt it wise not to contradict her. She struck him as a very disagreeable woman, like almost all the women his father took up with. It was obvious that he had no great talent for choosing women. That included his mother, of course.

"I don't choose women, son. They choose me," he protested once when they were talking about it.

"Why do you let them choose you?" he asked.

"I'm very tired," answered his father. "It's hard for me to stand up to them."

You could see at a glance that he had a hard time standing up to many things. That was why his father preferred to avoid trouble.

"Martha, we didn't mean to mock you," said his father, apologizing.

"My name isn't Martha. Quit making up stupid names for me. I have my own name, you jerk."

He could never quite remember the names of all the women, so whenever he met someone he would invent a new name for her, and he always tried to think of one that would fit his image of her better. It was easier to remember them that way: he would picture each with the name he had given her—but they weren't always pleased by the idea.

When they left the bar, his father was a little upset. He hadn't meant to make the woman angry.

"Don't worry," his son consoled him. "She's just pushy."

"Do you think so?" asked his father with a sigh of relief. It was terribly hard for him not to worry about all the men and women he met while he was out walking. Since he walked a fair amount every day, he worried a lot.

"What were you telling her?" his son asked on their way to the park. There was only one park in the entire city, and a strong southwester had leveled most of the trees, but even so, even with its sad air of devastation, he liked to sit there and talk. A few trunks still lay on the ground, with broken branches and dry leaves. It had been a powerful wind, that one, and it tore out the oldest roots easily, it sent roofs flying, it shook towers and broke antennas atop buildings.

"I was telling her about the time I was in Buenos Aires, when I won a fortune playing poker."

"You've never been to Buenos Aires," the boy told him. He hadn't been to Buenos Aires or any place else, except this impersonal city, because traveling terrified him, and besides he would never have been able to save enough money for the fare.

"Last night I dreamed I was in Buenos Aires, winning a fortune at poker. What do you think? If I had told her it was a dream, she would never have listened to me. Some people can't even remember their dreams. Their lives are terribly sad. How is Dino?"

"Oh, he's all right. He may come out on the beach tonight."

A dinosaur was always appearing in his dreams, clearly emerging from the waters, with large grey scales on its back, prominent scales like gigantic flower petals, its back raised, feet scraping the ground, its arms up, and a long, folding tail that moved forcefully. At first, its appearance (on a deserted beach. It is nighttime, or a crusty, dark afternoon, grey and lilac in tone, fish swimming violently on the surface of the water. It emerges from the waters as if the entire landscape has been preparing for its enormous eruption into air and space. It comes out slowly, and the waters, black and solid, scarcely move. Its huge, grey feet grasp the sandy bottom. Its arms, smaller, trap tiny human figures on the sand—like fish—it smashes their heads together and like empty hulls, like broken toys, it throws them back, into the oily center of the sea. It comes out ingenuously, innocently, without guilt. It emerges, immense and pure, like an enormous demented toy. Like a sick elephant. And playing with men is a benign, innocent pastime for it) filled him with trembling, and he woke up frightened, looking around, afraid the apparition would return, now, in the dark confines of his room. But little by little he grew accustomed to dreaming about it. He waited for it to appear in his dreams like a solemn, anachronistic ancestor. Like a friend wearing strange garb. Like a madman, like someone in exile who holds—in the depths of his madness—a trace of sadness and tenderness. He grew used to seeing it appear, to naming it, walking down the streets with it, having it for a companion and friend. He shared his day-to-day life with it, and even though no one could see it, it was there, although not always; sometimes it went back into the waters, for several days in a row he would go out walking and wouldn't find it at his side, nor did it haunt his room at night, and then one waited for it again, watching for it to appear on violet afternoons, in grey waters so solid that they don't seem to be water. Dino, ingenuous monster, and so familiar, a companion in the water, devourer of men, pursuer of fish; Dino, special friend, close relative with a strange physiognomy.

With the teacher, things weren't so simple.

When all the others had gone they went inside: she was arranging her notebooks and tablets in the great emptiness of the classroom. His father was reasonably sober ("Son, let me have a drink, just one, you don't know what it's like to be a father, I promise I won't get drunk, it's very hard to have so many responsibilities, I would never be able to face a teacher without a little drink to stiffen me up, someday you'll understand; just one, I tell you. All right, let's go."). He was smoking his pipe, and he looked at everything curiously. He hadn't been inside a school for years, he hadn't been in school since he was a child. Besides, he couldn't remember if he had even finished school. He would never be sure.

"*This* is your father?" the teacher exclaimed, emphasizing the pronoun, while looking disapprovingly at the ungainly bearded man in his threadbare shirt and suit, whose facial expression was more childish than the boy's.

"What a strange tree!" said his father, peering out the window at a brown, ash-colored tree. He was very fond of nature. The trees made him feel good; whenever he talked about a woman he would always say: "What I like about her is the wood." There were many different kinds of wood, and women.

"Miss," said his father very calmly. You could see that the drinks were having a positive influence on him. "Can you tell me what kind of tree that is?"

The woman had just looked him over. Duly, she gazed out the window: it looked like an ordinary tree to her, the kind you see everywhere.

"I don't know. A banana tree, I suppose. The street is full of banana trees."

"Absolutely not," responded his father, offended. "Are you trying to tell me that this is a plain, ordinary banana tree, the sort you can find anywhere? You're completely mistaken. Son, would you do me a favor and find out the name of that tree? I don't know what they can be teaching in this school if they don't even know the names of the trees here. And your name, please, what is it?"

The teacher seemed put out.

"My name is Sara."

"All right, Sonia, the fact of the matter is, I'm this boy's father. On that point, I won't take any criticism. I married when I was very young, it's true, just the way Christian society tells us to. I can't say for a fact that his conception was entirely deliberate, but then I'm not sorry about what fate had in store either. We could have waited a little longer or a little less, depending on how you look at it, but who knows how things might have turned out then. No one can really say they would have been better or worse. On the other hand, our happy marriage fell apart after four years, and that's not so long if you consider that the boy's entire conception lasted only nine months, and all that time my wife went around with a big stomach, she suffered from allergies, tonsillitis, nausea, and I found that I had to take a job. As you can see, he came out perfectly hatched. Besides, our papers are all in order. The child was baptized, he had three aunts and two uncles, four grandparents and only one sister, and despite all that, in general, he has wanted for nothing, as they say. Not even an extra father, a backup, which I'm sure you'll understand, since a boy's education is so difficult these days, and a woman's too. Two fathers are always better than none, wouldn't you say? And my wife can't stand to be alone. I must confess that I can't either. On the other hand, he still has only one mother. We didn't want to weigh him down with another one so soon."

The boy paid close attention to the conversation. He really enjoyed listening to his father. The second father, not as much. His father number one would obviously know how to write an essay.

"I'd really like to know who I would have been if I hadn't been me," declared the child.

Intrigued, the father looked at him for a moment. Then, at the teacher.

"Are you prepared to answer the boy, Sonia?" he immediately asked her .

"My name is not Sonia. It's Sara," protested the woman.

"That's not the point, Sonia. The boy just asked who he would have been if he hadn't been himself."

"I think I would have been someone else," the child finally answered.

"Exactly," said his father.

"So, in reality, I'm anyone," continued the boy. "Or I can try to be who I am. But it's hard to be the one you are if you know you could be somebody else."

"My son," the use of this form of address was the only thing the two fathers had in common, "I've been trying to be myself for precisely forty years, and even now I can't say with any real certainty that I've been successful."

"Then I could spend about forty years of my life trying to be anybody," proposed the boy.

"We could compare the results, and perhaps we could make a suitable arrangement, an exchange or something of the sort, don't you think? Let's not forget that we live in a market economy."

"It's also possible that if I hadn't been me, I would be absolutely no one."

"Or a tree with a name no one knows."

"A frog."

"A sunset."

"A son's sot."

"An eye."

"A ewe."

"Greased lightening."

"Grey sky."

"A spider."

"A tricycle wheel."

"A Bible."

"A TV set."

"A dream."

"Oh, yes, I could have been the dinosaur your son dreams about almost every night."

"And my son would be somebody else."

"Someone who wouldn't dream of dinosaurs."

"You could be a soccer ball in a stadium."

"Or your mother, wouldn't it be funny if I was your mother?"

"Or the teacher, if I were the teacher right now, what would happen?"

"I would have to give you good advice."

"You always give me that, even if you aren't my teacher."

"Other advice, when I give you advice, it's as your son, not as the teacher."

"This doesn't settle the matter of the tree. I can see, dear lady, that this school doesn't have the proper personnel. In the first place, they don't know what kind of trees they have around here. In the second place, you're not prepared to give my son—your student—a reasonable method for discovering who he would be if he weren't himself. So what sorts of things are you prepared to teach him?"

He took advantage of his father's speech to take out his pen and draw on the back of a chair. He did it surreptitiously, the way you have to do these things. He couldn't think of anything better to draw than a swastika.

They left the school together. His father was walking along very proudly, puffing comfortably on his pipe.

"I don't know why that woman sent for me, anyway," he remarked with satisfaction. "I don't think she has a very clear idea about what's going on. What was she trying to tell me?"

"She's trying to find out who the damned son of a bitch is that's been carving swastikas into the chairs. She's worried about the furniture, not the symbol," he said.

When he got home he said hello to his mother, and made the announcement:

"Jonah will be late for dinner. He's giving a demonstration about the future of machines for people who haven't put a cable in their head yet."

His mother looked at him, unruffled. She was used to her son giving his stepfather the first name that popped into his head. As for the meaning of his words, that was something she had decided not to delve into. At a very young age she had married a madman, and this was what she got for not knowing in time. People ought to carry around a mental health card so they can avoid these disasters. She, a young, inexperienced girl, had fallen prey to the delirium of a madman, and the child seemed to have inherited his father's worst traits. Fortunately, her second husband backed her up completely, he never said one word against her, and he was willing to spend time finding a cure for the child's mental problems, if that was even possible.

He found his sister lying down, staring at the ceiling. That was her favorite pastime whenever she wasn't reading.

"What are you up to today?" he asked her, sitting on the edge of the bed.

"Listen to this: in-tent, imp-lore, can-died, cap-rice, anchor-age, as-certain, bad-in-age, boo-king, grim-mace, to-get-her, end-ear, cur-tail, proper-ties, fabric-ate, car-nation, ear-nest, has-sock, bat-ten..."

"Have you been going through the dictionary again?"

"Yes. I'm going to ask Poppa to buy the Encyclopaedia Britannica. It must be a lot of fun."

"You don't even know English. You're not much more than an Indian."

"So much the better."

"Do you think it will match the emerald sofas?"

"Maybe the Encyclopaedia Britannica comes in different colors, you might be able to get it in colors to match the living room furniture and the carpets."

"I doubt it. The English are very traditional."

"So is Momma, but she has emerald sofas."

"Tradition isn't the same thing in one place as it is in another."

"Then I don't get what kind of tradition they're talking about."

"A tradition that's transitional."

"Transformational."

"Informational."

"Philosophical."

"Phonological."

"Pathological."

"Palestinian, Pasolinian."

"I don't know what that is."

"Neither does poppa."

"Which one?"

"This one."

"They won."

"Day one."

"Day-ton."

"Stop it."

"Stamp it."

"Tramp it."

"Trumpet."

"Strumpet."

"This morning Mama called the doctor and told him she thought we were too preoccupied with language."

"She's very preoccupied with our preoccupation with language."

"That's one of her pre-occupations."

"A dissi-pation."

"A dis-pensation."

"Did he prescribe medicine or the sea?"

"Sea."

"So."

"Sew?"

"Sow."

"What a man sows, that shall he reap."

"Give me liberty or give me death."

"Actions speak louder than words."
"Who pays the piper, calls the tune."
"Charleston."
"Heston."
"Chaps."
"Che."
"China."
"Choke."
"Check."
"Chancre."
"Chile yes, Yankees no."
"Con-sign."
"Con-science."
"Conciliate."
"Contempt."
"Content."
"Continent."
"Con-cord."
"Con-tour."
"Con-verse-station."
"Con-done."
"Con-dition."
"Con-fluent."
"I'll go down to the beach to con-sort with you."

There was a time when he had first dreamed of the dinosaur, but he couldn't remember when. His memory played tricks on him. What would happen if we could remember everything? Absolutely everything. A dinosaur that always came out of the sea, the dinosaur all silvery, the sea a dark blue. It came out of the waters, immense. When he tried to remember, it was already out. He could see its head very well, its feet were still in the water. He would go down to the beach afterward, and although he couldn't find its tracks, the sea had a dark blue color that almost wasn't blue now, but nearly black, and the sea was very low, very flat, very silent, as though nothing could come out of it, but the sky had the color of augury, the color of portent, as if all that calm held danger. The beach was deserted, and he waited for the offering from the sea. Conches, pieces of wood, empty shells (so he could listen to the echo of the sea, resounding through the nights), dead fish, and occasionally a sick wolf, come to die on the coast.

Dark lilac of the clouds, and the shoreline empty, on the sand the tiny, well-marked prints of gulls and other birds. The birds were not afraid. Not of him, or of the dinosaur. The birds remained in place, positioned on the sand, their eyes fixed on the low, very flat, very quiet sea. The birds were like statues of birds. And if they moved, they left patterns in the sand. All the boats had been pulled out of the water, and upside down they looked like nutshells. Then he sat down near the hill, to wait. In the dream the dinosaur came out at unpredictable times. Sometimes it seemed like dusk to him, other times it felt like dawn, even before the sun had come out. Be that as it may, what is certain is that no one was waiting for it, except him. Only he saw it, enormous, innocent, coming out of the waters, apparently dry, looking for people to play with. In the dream, the dinosaur came out at unpredictable times. The wait filled him with anxiety. He didn't know why, but he felt a need to control it. All that strength and power, loose in the world, was dangerous. Only he could see it from a distance, talk to it, stop its enormous arms from wrapping around people, impulsively knocking their heads together, then throwing them far away, deep into the ocean, where defeated ships sleep quietly. Ancient ships. The ships of old hunters of brontosauric whales. That was why he went down to the sea every afternoon, and sometimes in the morning, when the day was especially grey. It was his duty to stop it. To calm it. To tame it. To stop the destruction. To keep it from trapping his father, his sister, his friends. Watch for it to appear, standing guard at the rim of the sea, next to the waves, waiting for it to appear at any moment, like a revelation. He also had to stop everyone from finding and killing it. It was a very delicate mission. He was certain that if anyone saw it, they would destroy it, do away with it, thinking that the dinosaur would attack them. Or simply because they were used to killing. His task was difficult. He had to stop the annihilation of one by the others or of the others by one. Whom to take care of first? Because of his doubts he was always in the dark, but without concealing himself, because he thought it would be disloyal to be hiding. And he waited for it. He waited for it anxiously, in agony. He wasn't afraid for himself. The dinosaur would do nothing to him. They were good friends. It invaded him without permission, that's true, but he had grown so accustomed to its nocturnal irruptions, to its somnambulant appearance in the dream, that it was like a beloved ancestor, a legendary grandfather, a Norwegian sailor, run aground on the island of the dream. A friend somewhat eccentric in his ways, but whom we end up loving and esteeming. But he could not lose its confidence. He knew that sometime— while he was awake—the dinosaur would appear and carry out the terrible threat of the dreams, crashing onto the dark, blackened beach with its silvery sheen of fins and scales, fiercely squeezing the ingenuous inhabitants of this overpopulated planet in its arms. He especially wanted to protect his father number one, and his only sister; him, because he was incapable of taking care of himself, always mixed up with women who were rather dumb, rather ugly; his sister, because she was small and tender.

He saw it coming from a distance, and he shivered with cold. The night was dark. He could see the green flash from the main lighthouse far away, then the red one five seconds later. What surprised him most was that the coloring of its scales was exactly the same as it had been in his dreams. Grey and silvery, with a very intense sheen. It emerged slowly. As if meditating, or as if leaving the sea (a curious baby in its portable tub) were a delicate operation that had to be carried out with great care. Like a child who begins to walk uncertainly, and looks at the movements of its legs, and its feet and its arms, both astonished and pleased, and appraises the different pieces of its body separately, like parts of a strange and marvelous mechanism whose secrets we have just come to know. As if coming out of the water were a task it needed to be trained for. He watched it move one of its enormous, grey feet, slowly, as though exploring the fragile, slick territory of the sea—it imagined that its foot would be full of appendages of sea life, aquatic polyps, algae, plant-life, lichens and seaweed—as if that movement was its first, its back raised slightly, its head held high. First one foot, then the other. It recognized the second movement, it was astonished that it was identical, that this foot also, like a porous net, was scooping up those relics of the sea, the way a sucker traps objects in the water, green and full of froth, things that become attached like a polyp. It was startled that it could move over the sea, could lift the stony crust of its back. Like a child who takes his first steps, but in the midst of a fragile, watery, sticky territory. But once it has begun its march, its movements are more agile, considering its heavy bone structure, its body made of stone, mud, polished rocks, calcareous protuberances and slime.

It came out enormously, silently.

He waited for it, concentrating all his energy on looking, waiting, but trembling. What night was this mad night of revelations? A night like a narrow passage. A night like a black anthill. He trusted that he would not hesitate.

And when the enormous apparition,

silent,

the apocalyptic brontosaurus was near, he looked silently toward the house and cried out:

"Poppa!"

QUEEN'S GAMBIT

In the great hall with heavy crimson curtains and red carpets, Ceron was playing the lute, rendering a song that his friend Villon had composed for him:

> *Ou sont les gracïeux galans*
> *Que je suivoye ou temps jadiz,*
> *Si bien chantans, si bien parlans,*
> *Sy plaisans en faiz et en diz?*

The birds were resting on their perches, scarcely moving their heads, and the pupils of the motionless gyrfalcons widened in moist fury. Alexandra was intoxicating her animals in order to make them more perverse, more lustful. Play on, Ceron, play. As long as you play there will be music and life in the castle; Alexandra will stroll through the lighted halls, sowing life and death to the left and to the right, the servants will open the doors to the inner rooms, the wine cellars, bloody cellars, and peacocks will spread their fans as they strut under the light of the lamps, artificial sun, artificial daylight, because Alexandra cannot endure the night, the night frightens her as though she were a little girl disturbed at the moment she stops being a child, and silently, treacherously begins to be a woman, for one is born a child and one becomes a woman in a scandal of blood between the sheets. Play Ceron, play your enchanted cithara beneath the artificial light of the lamps that emulate a zenith now gone; with your lute, cloak a night that has already begun; as long as the fingers of Ceron do not grow weary, there will be daylight in the palace, there will be music, Alexandra will stroll through the columns and patios of her favorite halls, and a concert of lovers, chosen for the color of their skin, will make love so Alexandra will forget that it is nighttime and that her childhood was left behind, once, in a bed, in a helpless spurting of blood.

"Vitruvius, I wish I had been born a man, and that the only blood spattering my clothing was from dead rivals or from my own death the moment I died."

"Alexandra, I am not Vitruvius the poet, at one time I was a shepherd, not fully enough to be only a shepherd, I am one who stopped being a poet and a shepherd to become a warrior, not warrior enough as to stop being a poet or for you to stop being a queen."

"Tell me the story of the bees, Vitruvius, or this will be the last night of your life, of my life. Do you know the punishment for seditious warriors?"

"Not warrior enough, Alexandra, as to quit being a poet, as to quit being a shepherd. And not poet enough to keep from being a warrior."

"I have known many poets, Vitruvius, but although their verses were not as fine as yours, they never gave up the blue goose quill for the handle of a sword. They never left the goose for the sword. And their verses, Vitruvius, were not as fine as yours. But your sin is ambition. You should have stopped being something in life, Vitruvius, so that you could become something. And your ambition is responsible for the death in you of the poet, the warrior, and the shepherd of flocks, all of them at once. In you, three are dying, Vitruvius, in you I am killing three of my best courtiers, and that is too much, even for a queen."

"I was once a shepherd, and I lost sheep because of the verses, and I swear that I suffered as bitterly for the lost sheep as I did for the verses I did not write as a shepherd. I was once a warrior, and because of the wars I lost sheep, I lost verses, and I swear that I suffered for every verse, for every sheep, as much as for every enemy I did not kill. And the more I waged war, the more I wanted to care for the sheep, to write verses, and the more verses I wrote and sheep I took care of, the more I wanted to wage war. But Alexandra, your people killed our sheep, our flocks fled— scattering through fields the coloring of your wine cellars, and your soldiers amused themselves in our houses, raping the women as though they were our sheep. Your kind killed poets before they were born, before they could begin to write poetry, and one time, remembering and forgetting that I was a shepherd poet, I became a warrior, to protect the sheep, to save the poets."

"Vitruvius, tell me the story of the bees and we will do combat once again, at the chessboard, and perhaps your life will last one more night, until tomorrow, when day is here, when I am happy again, and you will be able to stroll through the palace gardens and gaze out upon the peacefulness of the parks, the rare trees, the geese gliding slowly over the lake."

"The silent geese moving slowly through the water. The soft murmur of the waterfalls. A lake, so calm, so serene, Alexandra, that you can hear the noise of open flowers as they fall, as they let go the branches and flee, swirling through the air until they brush against its surface. A lake so clear, Alexandra, that when I looked at myself in its waters, I could see a poet with a crown of faded laurel, sadly brandishing a sword, and I could see a dull shepherd letting his sheep wander off while he was writing verses, and I saw—in the clear waters of the lake I saw—a somnambulant warrior counting sheep, by the light of the fires. And the poems were lost in the water, and the sword moldered, and the sheep fled into the mountain. A poet of somber waters, a somnambulant shepherd, a warrior who pursues sheep. Not so much a warrior, Alexandra, as to quit being a poet, as to destroy you. This is the melancholy story of false shepherds, of sad poets, of warriors who lose wars. And every time you speak, I shudder, for you are mistress of all things I love—you, without loving them ever—sheep that graze in the fields, fields full of trees, trees where birds come to rest, the birds you command to be killed or spared, poets who will write no verses because they died before they could become poets."

"Vitruvius, complaints are useless. Let them die on the points of effete lances, and speak to me of the life of bees. Their sweet pollen. The honey they sip while they hover. Yes, them: with their dark brown stingers, bitter as gall, they might endure the anguishing solitude of night, when everyone departs and lights are extinguished. Explain to me, Vitruvius, why the night is barren, why the faces of friends turn strange and I can no longer recognize father or mother."

"There were many poets among us, Alexandra, many valiant warriors. And many shepherds who abandoned their sheep, exchanging their staff for a sword. And I left my dog behind, and when I turned back to look for him, your soldiers were surrounding him, surrounding me. He was a good dog, Alexandra, who fell behind on the road because he was old, because he was sick, and he returned sadly to his shelter; I could not leave him to the perversity of your soldiers."

"You should have abandoned him, Vitruvius. What is a dog, after all? You would have found others as you went your way, but you are not a good soldier. An able soldier does not turn back, over an uncertain road, to look for a dog that was left behind. You are not a good poet, Vitruvius. A good poet does not write verses on the blue edge of a sword. You are not a good shepherd, Vitruvius, a good shepherd does not leave a lost sheep so that he can write a verse."

"While we were fleeing, the dog fell back, tired, and I would not leave him to the atrocities of your soldiers. For whom could I fight, if I was not capable of protecting my dog?"

"Good warriors, Vitruvius, do not confuse war with love. When they fight, they forget love, even if, when they love, they don't always forget war. But one who loves sheep the same way he loves verses, the way he loves the sword, will die of forgotten sheep, of unwritten poems, of lost battles. A sad destiny, Vitruvius, for a man who wanted to be all three at once."

"No, Alexandra, I wanted to be only God, to be God. Nothing less! Not your palace with its still lakes where silent geese glide past, not the lustful trembling of the restless gyrfalcons, not your wandering, as a sleepless follower of Bacchus, through the sacrilegious halls of the palace. Not your decision to allow birds to live, to kill dogs, to stop poets from growing up, nor your all-consuming desire to be a man and to carry a sword between your legs."

"Tell me that story, Vitruvius, and for one more night you will see the slow, silent geese slip over the lake, and Ceron will play the lute, and the ephebic girl-boy, the ephebic boy-girl will come sit at our feet on the deerskin rug, and I will let you love her as I look on."

"I do not want the girl-tree now, the ephebic virgin, the ephebic nymph, Mnasidika, who never ceases to look at you, who goes mad when you leave her, who slips on hemp sandals and girds herself with the Hebrew tunic so that you can violently tear it off and remove her sandals. Whose name is Hylas and who appears in the palace in shepherd's garb to caress you with the flute, who intones the wedding song and devours you with his eyes, spills wine on your breast, licks the depths of your belly, lets his flock rest in the thicket of your pubis."

"Then, Vitruvius, we will make love for you. In my garden, on the deerskin rug (the fawn that used to eat from your hand, Vitruvius, and that Mnasidika killed happily, because I asked her to), I will remove her clothes brazenly, slowly, while the torches burn, I will run my hands over her body, slowly I will unfasten her clothing, I will let the tunic—the color of juniper—fall, and I will show you her round, warm breasts, white as lotus blossoms, and, along my journey, the blue birth mark she bears on her belly, I will smash fruit against her body, leaving its ocher and purple mark, like umbilical goblets. And I will proclaim her intimacies aloud, I will surprise her, like a sleeping roe, awaken her violently, biting her and ordering her about. She, the gentle, complacent girl, the unresisting slave, will smother her cries in the deerskin rug, as in tall grass. And from her I will wring moans of pleasure and pain; Vitruvius, don't you desire complacent little girls who are slender as little boys and submissive as slave-girls, and who drink from springs, like spent stags?"

"I don't want your love-sick little girl, Alexandra, I don't want Mnasidika or the shepherd Hylas, tomorrow I want to see the geese once again, gliding slowly over the lake. Alexandra, let that little girl go, let her row across the lake, return her to her parents, don't urge her to kill the deer in the gardens of your house, or to make your captive warriors jealous."

"Oh, shepherd, tell me that story, tell it, poet, before morning is near, let it run like water from the forests. I want to hear it. I want to hear it while Hylas caresses me, devours me with his moist eyes, while I slowly remove her sashes; loosen her clothing, slide my fingers over her and hear the enervating murmur of the bees, ah, their libations, that perpetual hovering, circular, like desire. That desire you can no longer feel, Vitruvius, for you are a defeated warrior, a poet who did not write all the verses you could have, a shepherd whose sheep have gone astray."

That's true. Since the day you killed my dog, Alexandra, I have felt no desire. My dull sex no longer stands erect when Ceron plays the songs of Villon on the lute, and slow, gentle geese glide over the lake, white, still, tranquil. A useless sex, an ineffectual sword, a broken staff; the rustle of crimson curtains no longer makes me shiver, nor does the caress of your slave-girls' sandals over the dead fawn, nor the insinuating, silent thighs of your maidens, with their graceful lines, their long arms and kisses, their sharp nails and mauve nipples.

"The story of the bees, or the black widow spiders who devour the male after fornication?"

"Alexandra, in their savage state the bees lived in the clefts of rocks, in the trunks of trees or suspended from branches.

(We spent the greater part of the year in hiding. In caves, in caverns protected by vegetation where your soldiers did not enter, terrified by insects, entangled in twining vines, lost in the marshes, and the world, Alexandra, was favorable to us then, favorable the natural fruit of the trees, of the earth, favorable the rains that kept your armies from crossing the forest, favorable the dark night where no one dared venture. And you wandered through the patios of your palace, wrathful and violent, angry, pursuing the deer of your forest, compelling your soldiers to make love to you, or dragging your slave-girls, your friends, through the cellars.)

"Alexandra, the life of the hive depends on a perfect female with two large ovaries, the queen, while around her work and hum the sexless females and the drones."

(When you awaken, when you move, the earth begins to turn and activity multiplies, the hive hums and bustles, female workers come and go, you are sprawled on the bed, your head lying on the feather pillow that still bears the perfume of your men, of your women, and you have two full breasts that rise like mountains and two ovals between your legs, round and moist, like two open mouths. And inside of them, each comes to deposit its offering. Its tiny branch of laurel. Its pine. Its empty shell. Its white sugar. Its enervating liquor. Its burning honey. Its billy goat froth. The braid of its slave-girl. Its fragrant wine. The belt of its tunic. The powder of certain breasts. The impudicity of audacious laughter. The mouth of a little girl. The shepherd's staff. The poet's quill. The useless sword, Alexandra, since you had my dog put to death.)

"Each hive has only one fertile female, the queen, and around her the life of the colony turns."

Ah your bold demonstrations of power. That game you play with me each night, on the living board; one of the old ladies of your court represents the castle, and on the black flag-stone you position your best horse, the one you ride, naked, through the palace forest, and on the next is your favorite courtier, the one you choose for the size of his sex and his fire, but Alexandra, you will never lose the game, because you play without a king. You conquer me that way, night after night, since I can only give chase to your minor pieces, to your clumsy pawns who have not learned to play, I can even go up to the castle while you steal my fields, your soldiers violate my sheep, they enter my houses, they kill my horses and my bishops, and my helpless queen, the sad widow, flees, and hurls herself into the lake of silent geese. And you have won the game again.

"You have lost again, Vitruvius, my queen has conquered your queen. My queen has broken the neck of your king."

"And, overcome, the shaft of my antenna vibrates. And those defenseless males, deprived of their stinger, as am I, Alexandra, surrounded by your aggressive females, the ones who carry a barb in their abdomen, those males without glands, die at your side, apathetic and sickly."

"The queens use their mandibles, Alexandra, to cut through the doors of the cell, to reach the honey. And they have a tongue, Alexandra, that penetrates the interstice of the flower, breathing in the pollen the nectaries hold."

(Alexandra, leave that little girl alone. Let loose her tunic. Don't close your lips between her legs, let her run to the lake and feed the geese. Alexandra opens her mouth the way a crevice opens in the earth, with the same fury, the same avidity; her lips, two smooth, strong, agile spatulas, swallowing, devouring, in the sweet action of separating the skin, of tearing the membrane that hides the fruit, of closing brusquely, and pressing, of sucking what is hidden in its cell.)

"Mnasidika, I am the queen. I, the queen. And I want to enter, to slide along the smooth sides of your legs; to cut the sweet fabric, to gather the pollen, to reach the honey that you hide in your cell and to lick it with my tongue, with my lips, to inhale it slowly, deliberately. Then, when my tongue is swollen, I will furiously part the hair on your legs and I will withdraw the sweet and bitter fruit."

"Mnasidika, ephebic boy-girl, ephebic girl-boy, resist. Allow her to suck, but close your legs. In exchange, I will tell you a story of valiant warriors who suffered a siege until all were dead but one, all but the one who survived and who is now dying in the palace. Resist, Mnasidika. Let your cover of wax be so hard that the queen cannot cut it with her iron jaws. Mnasidika, close your cell. Fortify your wax. Set all the drones to point at her. Ah, those lazy drones who have never held a weapon."

"What is the end of the story, Vitruvius? Tell me."

"The queen has gone out on her rounds of fertilization. (Flee, Mnasidika, toward the lake. I will show you a secret road, the one shown to me by the geese that escaped death. Run away and don't come back, change your tunic, like the bees that abandon their hive, change your perfume, your hair, the way you walk and move.)"

"Vitruvius, you are a chaste man."

"On her nuptial journey, the queen goes through her rooms. She looks at the day dawning, radiant, she surprises the drones who are enjoying the light and warmth outside the palace. The queen leaves the palace slowly and lasciviously, she surveys the horizon, she makes her first flight of reconnaissance; the drones gather around her and inhale her odor of female in heat, they note the lustful vibration of her wings, an invitation for ejaculation, but disdainfully she flies over her males, observing their appearance, calculating their vigor."

"A delicious operation, that one, Vitruvius, a magnificent flight. And the chosen one, drunk with desire, lost forever, hurls himself outside, to attack he throws out his only member, a gigantic one, he transfixes her vagina, he stops up the narrow passageway, he fills all space, and the feminine ring closes in upon him, like a mouth clamped tight, she bites the sword, she truncates the poem; in vain, the male tries to free himself, she has closed her legs, leaving the vain inhabitant entrapped in her hair, and she furiously tears apart the intrusive organ, the projecting member. The warrior has died. In the struggle, he has lost his weapon. His trunk has been torn out. He dies, terrified, stripped of his strength.

"Then the queen returns to her palace. Her slave-girls anxiously await her at the door, waving their kerchiefs, intoning canticles, and Ceron plays the lute, Ceron, the castrated musician. The females wait for her, sprawled on the carpets, their white, moist, milky bellies vibrating like antennae. The queen descends and stops a moment to look at her maidens. She caresses their bellies, for a moment she licks their palpitating breasts. They welcome her, solicitously. They have adorned the palace with irises and lilies. A violent perfume, lubricous and heavy, permeates the halls. The servants follow her to her rooms, to help her remove her clothes and bathe, to strip off the residues of her journey. And it is all over, until the next day."

"Oh, Vitruvius, I wish I had been born a bee, had been a man. I would not have traded my sheep for a sword, my staff for the quill of a poet. And I would not have stopped to gaze at the slow, lazy drifting of geese on the lake."

And you, little Mnasidika, kill me. Because I was once a shepherd and I let the sheep stray so I could write verses, because as a poet I took up the sword and abandoned my verses. Because as a warrior I lost my sword, Mnasidika, and became a drone. Because I plunged my barb into the vagina of a queen, and Mnasidika, I continue to live, I go on living, in an endless nuptial copulation.

THE STORY OF PRINCE IGOR

And in his palace he kept women one thousand years old
who never died,
but breathed a rancid perfume
ancient and petulant
that contaminated the air of the hall
and the mirrors.
They played the harp, nonetheless,
and were able to dance.

He spent most of his time watching
their macabre dances.
His mother had died very young,
                              in childbirth,
and he called them "mama".

No one knew the secret of their long lives.

When they danced, their long grey tunics disintegrated like
dry leaves, crushed, and he had the servants pick up the
dust they left behind. Coming along with tiny brooms

made of fine maidens' hair, they swept the floor where the women danced.

They spent the greater part of the night dancing. As they moved
slowly, pausing,
clumsy by virtue of their advanced years,
their tunics fell apart. He ordered the servants to gather the dust they left
as a sign of their passing
and the servants placed what they had gathered in delicate, transparent coffers.

"What is strange," said Igor, "is that the dust they shed while they dance changes in color." In truth, as they danced they left behind a tenuous, very volatile trail, ephemeral, its specter running from grey to red. Whenever possible, they danced alone, with movements extremely slow and halting, dragging their clothing along the floor—as is normal for women of advanced years—but with great dignity. The nobility of the movements led Igor to believe that these were women of high lineage.

Although some obscene words that they were wont to repeat, as they moved slowly, very slowly—like heavy boats—across the strip, might have made him wonder if these were not really court ladies, preserved in time through some enchantment of the tribe's sorcerers.

In transparent coffers, the dust varied in color.

When he spoke to them, they did not answer, and this seemed to him a lack of courtesy and civility, but in deference to their advanced years he did not wish to punish them.

They wore no adornments, and all their tunics were grey.

Each coffer was inscribed with the name Igor had given each woman, the servants being extremely careful not to pour the dust they gathered into the wrong flask.

Some coffers had more dust, and some less,
which caused Igor to believe they did not all disintegrate in the same way.
But the surprising thing was, in spite of all the dust they left behind,
the women remained the same in appearance.

As if the dust they shed did not belong to them.
As if it were dust from something else.
As if they had nothing in common with the Holy Scriptures.

(Igor was an atheist.)
He spent a great deal of time pondering the dust in the flasks.
It hurt him that his mother had not been one of them, so that he could at least preserve her in a flask.

As he watched the noble ladies, the obscene ladies of the court, dancing all through the day, he neglected the affairs of state. As a result, the affairs of state went along rather well.

In addition to labels on the flasks, Igor decided to put a symbol on each of them. To him it seemed a courtesy, a way to repay these ladies, so he had various emblems engraved in copper and silver. To one he assigned a bow and lyre (due to a very visible defect of her nose), to another, a nautical rose, a sea rose (for her constant weeping), to another, a coin with her image (she liked to catch glimpses of herself in mirrors as she danced, to observe her heavy, senile movements), for the fourth he chose a trident (because she danced with a wooden leg), he honored the fifth with a cymbal (her bones creaked as she danced), and so on, down the line. When he tried to engrave the same symbols into their clothing, the palace artisans confessed their impotence: the tunics were of stone, a burin and hammer would be necessary, but Igor declined to damage their garments.

Woman Number One has a prominent, slightly bent nose. Igor thinks her ancestor was a bird. If she looks at him, it is with stern eyes, and Igor feels very small, very timid and stupid. He flies up to a tree in front of the window, and spies on her from there. Sibyl—Igor's sister—looks for him in the hall, but does not find him. With a haughty gesture, she drives the ladies from her path and makes the servants go in search of Igor. She thinks it a rather silly game, but she loves her brother very much, and will deny him nothing. Not even her hand, at night, when Igor appears in her chamber, his eyes brilliant with liquor, his clothing unfastened, after doing combat with his dreams, and lets himself fall upon the sheets, calling out to the women sweetly and imperiously. Not even her breast, when Igor furiously tears apart her clothing and allows the white cadaver of the dove he has just killed to fall onto the blue carpeting.

Then Sibyl finds him, and Igor is seated on the silver chest, his feet are enormous, his eyelashes and bones enormous, his tusks are enormous and his chest is very hard. Igor is sitting on the silver chest, and Sibyl is a very small girl.

Woman Number Two is very fond of crying. Igor thinks of the great abundance of tears she must have shed since she was born, thousands of years ago. Igor thinks that her tears have formed the seas, the rivers, the oceans and their currents. That they have sprung from the mountains and spilled torrents of water down upon the cities, swallowing up cattle, churches and castles. That she has rained or cried upon the masses and caused the rivers to overflow. That she has flooded the gardens. He has had a pit dug in the center of the palace patio, and would like her to cry into it so that the geese and swans might glide back and forth across its surface. He would like to preserve a lake of her tears. A canal of her waters.

Or a dream of her lake, says Sibyl. Sometimes Sibyl takes part in the game. Only sometimes, when she wants to rest from the affairs of state. Igor has ordered a dam built to hold the tears of Number Two. He thinks it is perfectly right that the affairs of state should be his sister's concerns, and that his own should be considerations of love and dance, of living and dying, of sleep and vigil.
Or a lake that is a dream. Or the dream that inhabits it, or the lake dissolved into tears, or the tears turned into a lake, turned into a dream. Sibyl dreams. Sibyl smiles. Sibyl lake spring dream goose inhabits swan, Igor of tears.
Igor looks at the plan for the dam and says yes. He is not entirely convinced that the dam will be large enough for all the water of Woman Number Two, but in any case, it will hold her tears for a few months, and for Igor time is never more than tomorrow.

For Sibyl, time is yesterday.

She gives orders to the ministers, and she runs the household. Someone must do it, says Sibyl, who is jealous of Number Two.   Igor has never shown as much enthusiasm for a dam as he has for this one.

Igor has had mirrors installed throughout the house. Different types of mirrors. There are round ones, like full moons nailed to the wall. Like moons that have slid by. Like moons that are propped up. They are tired moons, moons that have wandered off, roamed afar. They have ogival and rhomboid shapes. There are laminated mirrors, quicksilvered, burnished, double, triple, multiple mirrors, mirrors that deform, mirrors that enlarge and mirrors that diminish, flat or curved mirrors, cold mirrors and warm mirrors, concave and convex mirrors, mirrors that reflect and mirrors that conceal. There are mirrors like houses, and there are house-mirrors. Mirrors made for looking into and mirrors for being looked at. Igor has had them installed so that Woman Number Three can see herself. One day he discovered that when Number Three danced she liked to see her reflection.   At that moment he envisaged filling the palace with mirrors, in case she should want to see herself again at any moment.   Sibyl protests. She is tired of finding women throughout the house. When she gets up, when she moves, when she leaves one room and goes into another, she always finds women looking at her—like lesbians. It is difficult to go around all day, feeling that you are constantly being observed.

"Yesterday," says Sibyl, "when I got up, I heard a noise, and immediately I covered my pubis with my hand. It was a noise like mirrors breaking, shattering into small pieces, and when I took my hand away it was bloody. I ran to the nearest mirror to look at myself, and I saw you, Igor, smiling and drunk, embracing a maid. Be more discreet, I beg you. With so many mirrors in the house, it's very difficult to have any privacy. Besides, the maid was common."

Tomorrow Igor found Sibyl bloody, in a heap, in front of the mirror. He bent down to her, she was so small, he was afraid he might break her when he lifted her up. He called to one of his servants, a dwarf, and asked him to pick her up with all possible care, and lay her on a bed. The servant lifted her in his tiny arms and carried her to her chamber with great respect.
He lay her on the white sheets and left Igor alone with her. Igor was afraid of wounding her with his eyes, so he looked away, he picked up a clear, empty flask and very delicately—always keeping his eyes averted—he placed her inside. He closed the flask and summoned the courage to look at her. Sibyl was bleeding from her pubis, and he wanted to say sweet, tender words to her that would stop the flow of blood, but he saw that she could not hear him, enclosed as she was in the flask. Then he called the servant and asked him to place the flask next to the ones containing the dust the women shed as they danced.

"So much dust in the flasks, Igor, I think it's making us ill," said Sibyl yesterday. She was looking toward the gallery of transparent flasks that Igor was observing. There was fuchsia dust, ocher dust, gray dust, mallow dust and rose dust. "What are you hoping to see in it?" asked Sibyl, as she attempted to resist the fascination of looking. A woman of state cannot dedicate so much time to contemplation, while Igor, Igor can.
"If my mother had been one of these women," Igor said tomorrow, "we could still have her with us. We would have a flask with a little dust, that's true, Sibyl, but it's better than having nothing."

"In any case," said Sibyl, "it's better than having women dance all through the house, shedding dust."

"It's better than having nothing, tomorrow tomorrow," said Igor.

"But it was that way yesterday and yesterday," answered Sibyl. "You must accept it."

This morning Igor woke up, furious, because he had dreamed that a servant spilled a little dust from the flasks onto the carpet. He called the servant in and asked for an explanation. He called out to Sibyl and told her his dream. He wanted to punish the servant for his negligence. Sibyl told him that in dreams the dust, not the servants, is responsible for the flasks, in any case.

"It was always responsible dust," answered Igor. "It's possible to pick up dust that's been spilled," she suggested.

"It wouldn't be the same dust, it would be a mixture of dust, paltry dust, sick dust, a transmuted dust," asserted Igor.

The tiny bit of dust had fallen onto the ground and soiled the carpet.

"We could gather up the dream and confine it in the flask too, Igor," proposed Sibyl. He was disturbed yesterday and did not accept solutions easily.

"I would need another servant to watch over the flask with the dream inside," Igor objected.

"Was it a restless dream, very young, constantly roving?" asked Sibyl.

"A dream is always a dream, and I won't allow a clumsy servant to let it escape," protested Igor.

Finally Sibyl put the dream into a flask herself. That way Igor would be more at ease, and he would not suffer because of the lost dust.

"The problem," Igor said tomorrow, "is that if I dream the same dream again, I won't know if it's a mirror of the dreamed dream, if it's the dream that wandered off while I was sleeping, or if it's the dream that escaped from the flask."

Sibyl reflected. The art of governing the state left her entirely free to meditate. She had discovered that she could direct the affairs of the kingdom in her imagination, and as a result she did not need to do anything, and dedicated herself to resolve the problems of Igor, who, as a state, was much more difficult to govern. After a short while, Sibyl found the solution: they would put a mirror in front of the dream to keep watch over it at all times, so that they would always know if the dream was inside the flask or if it had escaped. To find out, Igor would have only to look at the mirror.

That night Igor dreamed of a mirror that reflected a mirror where there was a flask with a dream inside, which, since it was glass, reflected a mirror that reflected a mirror, where there was a flask with a dream inside, which, since it was glass, reflected a mirror that reflected a mirror, where there was a flask with a dream inside, which, since it was glass, reflected a mirror, that reflected a mirror, where there was a flask with a dream inside, which, since it was gla...

Igor got up, he began to run through the palace, he crossed the galleries, he went into his sister's room.

"Sibyl," he said, "please wake me up, the mirror guarding the flask with a dream inside has just dreamed me."

With a very white, very soft sheet, Sibyl very sweetly covered the bare breasts of the maid sleeping next to her, and looked around. Her eyes wandered over the paintings in the room, the carpets, the curtains, they returned to the naked body of the maid who was asleep, and quickly—with the speed and cunning of a bird of prey—she shattered the flask with a poker. Then Igor awoke and was able to go back inside the mirror.

The dream slipped, and went back into the mirror, this was the dust Igor had been pursuing.

Woman Number Four has a wooden leg, and when she dances, she moves it very slowly. She pulls up her dress to display the wooden leg better, and takes a few quick, firm steps that make a toc toc sound when they hit the floor. Toc one, toc two, toc to the left, toc to the right, toc in front, toc in back. Number Four's dancing fascinates Igor, and he would like to applaud her every movement if he weren't afraid of breaking the dancer's concentration. Because she is concentrating solely on what she is doing. She keeps her eyes down, and is always looking at the brown club that appears under her dress. The other leg is a normal leg, flesh, with its slight, rosy color, and its foot with five toes, plus five well-trimmed nails hidden by her sandal. But the other leg has no sandal, it ends in a wooden stump that pounds on the floor as she dances. Igor has made a considerate gesture: carelessly, as though it were unplanned, he left a pair of crutches on a chair within reach of Number Four. At first she seemed not to notice them, but when Igor discreetly left the room to observe her in a mirror hidden among the curtains, he saw her go, in the middle of the dance, to the seat with the crutches, and without a pause in her dance steps, she took them in her hands, propped them against the floor, and holding them under her arms, she began to dance with them. Now the toc toc was twice as loud, and it affected Igor deeply. She danced very skillfully, moving the crutches through the air as though they were oars, wooden wings, resting here—poc—resting there—poc—rising, descending, and Igor saw that the dust she was leaving behind had now changed color. The dance reached a climax when she opened her two wooden legs, making a perfect line, and began to beat the two ends of the crutches against the floor as though sending a coded message.

Igor has spent several mornings deciphering the coded signals Number Four sends out with her wooden legs.

Sibyl is disturbed by the pounding of crutches in the palace hall. She says it makes it hard for her to imagine the affairs of state.

Igor has summoned diviners to the palace.

Igor has consulted ciphered oracles.

Number Four continues to pound on the floor.

Wondering what it could mean, Igor neglects his dreams that create dust.

Abou Maschar Dejafar Ibn Mohammed, also named Albumazar, an expert in astrology and disciple of Alchindius The Philosopher, has arrived at court. Sibyl has protested this advent. She is certain that the time of dreams does not coincide, and she asserts that the disciple of Alchindius is an impostor.

"The dream of Number Four dancing corresponds to the 12th century, Igor, and Abou Maschar Dejafar Ibn Mohammed was born in the 9th century."

"You are mistaken, sister," Igor has replied. "Albumazar showed me that it wasn't really I who dreamed dancer Number Four pounding on the floor with her wooden leg, but himself. He was already an old man when, one long summer's night perfumed with jasmine and sandalwood, by the light of a candle and after consulting mysterious old manuscripts, he dreamed the invalid dancer, and he was kindled with an unhappy love for her, being unloved in return, and unable to eat or sleep, unable to read or travel, unable to console himself by reading old papyruses, for without her he could do nothing, he pursued her through forests, across rivers, brooks and mountains; she ran before him, always, because although she was in truth an invalid, he was already very old—as though the ancient manuscripts weighed down upon him—and running through meadowland and plains, she continued to beat on roots, rocks, the bark of trees, calling out for help, and someone must have given it to her, the master maintains that someone helped her, because one night she managed to escape Albumazar's dream, and the poor old man never heard of her again, until I summoned him into my own dream. So, in fact, he was the first to dream her, but once she had escaped the boundaries of this man's dream, she dreamed me, as I try, in vain, to decipher the meaning of her messages."

"It's strange," said Sibyl. "Now I'm not really sure if it was she who dreamed you, or if you dreamed her, or if the old man dreamed the two of you. So, now what will you do, Igor?   Will you return her to her first master/dream?" asked Sibyl, anxious for solutions.

Igor thought a while. While he was thinking, all the machinery of the dream stopped moving, the dance was left unfinished, the women, contorted in difficult dance positions, the lights burning, all movement stopped. Although no one was able to utter a single word, Igor knew that it was not good to draw out the time he was meditating for very long, because it worried him to see the forced and often uncomfortable positions in which he had frozen the people.

After reflecting a while, Igor came to a decision. He had all the curtains drawn, the rooms closed, the lights extinguished, and he retreated into one of his chambers, and taking several Equanil tablets, he decided to go to sleep.   Once he was asleep, he ordered a servant to introduce Albumazar into his dream, and all night long Igor dreamed of an ancient astrologer dressed in long robes, moving very slowly, in love with an invalid dancer who ran before the old man, hopping on her wooden foot, while the distance between them always remained the same, they would again pass by the same locales, by the great stone washing places, by the spring where the maiden was raped, by the cathedral of St. Petersburg, by le Bois de Boulogne, the woman made signals, with her wooden leg she beat on the bark, the tree trunks, the walls, she left footprints, marks, she made holes in the ground, the old man pursued her with difficulty, but without falling back, without stopping, she showed signs of fatigue, and when she reached the edge of a gentle and ritual lake like a mirror, she stepped into it immediately, so that she disappeared from the dream, and Igor awoke.

It is the archeologist's task to permanently reconstruct the bone-structure of Woman Number Five, which comes apart while she dances. At first Igor was very gracious, and every time a tibia or a femur, an occipital or a cornea, a bone from her head or a shoulder blade fell to the floor, he bent down ceremoniously, picked it up carefully with his hands and returned it to its rightful owner the moment a dance step brought her close to him. Always looking straight ahead, she took the piece haughtily, as though nothing had happened—which, in a way, was true—and stuck it quickly under her dress: Igor did not know if that swift, decorous movement was able to put the disjoined piece back in its proper place, or if, in fact, she had a coffer full of bones and unhinged pieces beneath her dress. Out of simple decency, he did not allow himself to lift her dress and look underneath, but he was afraid that any moment, while he was gone, a fundamental part would fall off, or an important bone would break or separate and—without anyone coming to pick it up from the floor—the thousand-year-old lady would fall, would collapse, what a crash, like a wounded bird, a curtain dropping from the ceiling. When the poor lady made her first mistake, Igor decided to hire an archaeologist. It was Sibyl who brought him the sad news.

"Igor, I think Number Five has made a slight error," she told him one day, before he went into the dance hall. Indeed, during his absence, one of her shinbones had fallen to the floor with a great clatter. The servant came quickly, picked up the bone and very courteously held it out to the lady who, as she passed, whirling in her endless dance before the dwarf, took it in her hands and attached it to her shoulder blade. As she entered the hall, Sibyl was able to view the strange spectacle of Number Five dancing clumsily, a bone sticking out at the height of her shoulders, like a top tilting to one side that at any moment will stop spinning, will wobble, and will fall over in a faint.

That day Igor hired the archaeologist, who remained in the hall to reconstruct Woman Number Five whenever one of her parts fell to the ground. He wasn't entirely pleased, because he couldn't bear the thought of a stranger handling the ladies. It depressed him to think that the archaeologist was touching her.

At this time Sibyl let her mind wander, imagining a problem of state. She imagined a rebellion so that Igor would be forced to leave the hall of the thousand-year-old ladies. She imagined it so strongly that a real upheaval of rebellious peasants soon broke out in the kingdom, and they occupied the territories that belonged to the landholding class. This created a great scandal among the landholders who were far away from their properties, enjoying the prosperity that comes with the possession of properties. They were in Nice on their yachts, on the Cote d'Azur, basking in the sun, in the Casino at Monte Carlo, gambling unconcerned, or they were touring the barbaric, highly exotic countries of America. Sibyl imagined this dream so strongly that one morning Igor awoke and quickly went into Sibyl's room. He pushed aside the dogs that guarded the entryway to the room, and when he was inside he had all the maids who shared his sister's bed leave.

"Sibyl," cried Igor in anguish, throwing himself upon the sheets that the maids had left free. "I dreamt that the peasants in the East were rebelling, and had taken possession of the lands that belong to their lords."

Sibyl looked at him and said nothing. Her body had increased greatly in size; through her open dressing-gown, Igor was able to gaze upon her enormous breasts like incandescent mountains, and while he spoke to her his eyes remained fixed on the declines and plains of the two hills. Sibyl stretched her entire body. Igor saw serpents entangled in the sheets, he saw a very young lion creeping around her waist, he saw a dark cavern where gazelles were hiding, he saw a swan gliding past, he saw a panther awaken and stretch its limbs, he saw two alligators stretched out in the sun. He saw himself as a mountain climber, ascending from the plains. The hill was very high, and he climbed eagerly, infinitely smaller and less hindered; he threw up a rope that caught on a distant peak at the summit, and holding it tightly, he painfully hoisted himself a few meters, grazing his face and body against the sides of the mountain. It was a blue mountain, furrowed with small currents of water like veins, and green vegetation like algae. The ascent was difficult and slow. The mountain had crags and peaks, savage trees, at times he was able to reach a place, but against his will he was dislodged, he slipped, he fell, he slid back; it was not firm, uncluttered territory. Igor was constant, however, and persevering: the rope flew into the air once again, it snared a peak, he held himself up, indestructible, from the terrain he had conquered, Sibyl's legs were firm, he was able to climb boldly, when he had hold of her hips he was able to ascend more easily, he climbed with his legs and his hands and with his tongue and with his fingernails and with his feet, at times a carelessness on the part of Sibyl caused him to fall back, but not much, an abrupt movement, not fleeing, a slip of her soft thighs, of her yielding sides, but he held himself straight, firm, without letting go of the sides of the mountain. Occasionally he stopped to drink from a spring, then he continued his painful ascent. He climbed, seemingly indifferent to the shuddering of the volcano at the summit, whose lava enveloped him. The lava flowed down and burned the skin on his arms and legs. A solid, incandescent, lethal lava, invading the threshed fields, the cultivated flatlands, the well-known lakes. When he reached the top, Sibyl informed him:

"Igor, you should do battle next to me."

But it was already too late, for the rebellious peasants had reached the gates of Igor's dreams; with lances, pikes, stones and clubs they beat on the windows, they lashed at the walls, the broke down the ramparts, and Igor realized that they would enter his dream and displace the dancing ladies.

"Sibyl, I'm dying," groaned Igor. But with the noise the doors of Igor's dreams were making as they fell in, Sibyl selected two of her favorite maids from her cortege, and quickly fled. When the three women heard the pounding very close to Igor's room, they went into the mirror, and Sibyl looked one last time at Igor,

who was dreaming that Sibyl had fled with her favorites into a mirror.

SIMULACRUM II

For ten days we had been orbiting the moon. On either side of the hatch we could see only the intense, infinite, universal blue of space. We felt no heat, no cold. We experienced neither hunger nor thirst. We suffered no confusion, no illness of any kind. Our hair did not bother us, nor did our teeth. There was no dark, no light. We cast no shadow. When asleep, we did not dream. In this place there was neither nightfall nor dawn. Only the full moon, always. No clocks, no photographs. We could sleep, or remain awake. No one dressed, no one undressed.

After ten days, Silvio begged me to tell him a story. But I could remember nothing.

"Make something up," he pleaded. But in the sterility of space, forever winding around the moon, I could invent nothing.

"Talk to me," he said then. I searched for a word written on some part of the ship, one that I could speak aloud. In vain: machines no longer needed instructions: they worked autonomously. No words anywhere for me to read. Only the endless blue of space on either side of the hatch. We felt no heat, no cold. We experienced neither hunger nor thirst. We suffered no confusion, no illness of any kind. There was neither darkness, nor shadow.

Sounds were faint, weak, attenuated. We did not need to lie down, or to stand. We could sleep, or remain awake. No one dressed, no one undressed.

Finally, with all the strength I could gather, I managed to speak one word:

"Mercy," I said.

ABOUT THE AUTHOR

Born in Uruguay in 1941, Cristina Peri Rossi is considered one of the leading Latin American writers in prose and poetry of the post-boom generation (that of Gabriel García Márquez, Mario Vargas Llosa, Carlos Fuentes and Julio Cortázar). Exiled to Spain (due to her political activities against the military dictatorship of Uruguay in the 1970's), she has written more than thirty works that emphasize her concern with all forms of repressive cultural practices limiting individual freedom. Well-known for her defense of civil liberties and freedom of expression, she has long supported gay marriage. Her works have been translated into more than fifteen languages.

THE TRANSLATORS

Robert S. Rudder received his Ph.D. in Spanish from the University of Minnesota. Gloria Arjona received her Ph.D. in Spanish from the University of Southern California. They have both taught Spanish language and literature at several universities in the United States, and have translated a number of literary works from Spanish to English.